The Fairy Kitten

...and other stories

Bounty
Books

Published in 2014 by Bounty Books,
a division of Octopus Publishing Group Ltd,
Endeavour House,
189 Shaftesbury Avenue,
London WC2H 8JY
www.octopusbooks.co.uk

An Hachette UK Company
www.hachette.co.uk
Enid Blyton ® Text copyright © 2014 Hodder & Stoughton Ltd.
Illustrations copyright © 2014 Octopus Publishing Group Ltd.
Layout copyright © 2014 Octopus Publishing Group Ltd.

Illustrated by Maggie Downer.

ISBN: 978-0-75372-642-6

A CIP catalogue record for this book is available from the
British Library.

Printed and bound by CPI Group (UK) Ltd, Croydon, CR0 4YY

CONTENTS

The
Fairy Kitten

There was once a little boy called John.
He lived with his mother and father in a
lovely little cottage at the edge of the
woods. Usually he was a happy little boy,
who laughed and played all day in the
sunshine, but just lately he had been very
unhappy because his little grey kitten
had run away and got lost.

John had looked everywhere for her –
in the house, in the garden, in the
summerhouse, in the garage and in the
road.

"She may have run into the wood,"
said his mother. "Go and see if you can
find her there, John."

So off John went to the woods where
primroses and celandines were flowering,
and where the silver pussy-willow shone

pale and soft in the warm spring sun.

But his kitten was nowhere to be found, and John could have cried with disappointment. He had so loved playing with her. He was sure he would never find another kitten that was as pretty as she was.

Suddenly he stopped still and listened. Was that a mew that he heard? Surely it was!

The noise came again softly, very high and quiet, not exactly like a mew, but John couldn't think what else it could be. He began looking about to see where the noise came from. It sounded as though it came from somewhere low down.

Yes, it came from the middle of a prickly gorse bush! Surely his poor little kitty couldn't be in there.

"Kitty! Kitty!" he called, peeping into the bush.

A little high voice answered him. "Oh, help me, please. I'm caught in the prickles!"

John was so surprised to hear the tiny

voice that he could hardly speak. "Who are you?" he asked at last.

"I'm a pixie-piper," said the little voice. "The wind blew me right off my feet and landed me here, and I can't get out! Will you help me?"

"A pixie!" John said excitedly. "Yes, I'll help you! I've never seen a pixie before! But, oh my! It's rather prickly!"

He put his hands right into the gorse bush and pressed back the branches. There, in the middle, was a tiny pixie, dressed in red and yellow. Carefully John

lifted him out of the bush and set him down on the ground.

"Oh, thank you!" cried the pixie. "You are kind to help me, but look at your poor hands. They are covered in scratches and scrapes. And why do you look so unhappy?"

"I'm upset because I've lost my kitten," John said sadly, and told the little pixie all about it.

"Dear, dear, that's very sad!" said the pixie-piper. "But don't worry, I'll help you. I think I know where your kitten may be. The fairies love kittens. If they've found yours, they'll have changed her into a fairy kitten. She won't be very far away. But we will have to use some pixie magic to find her. Have you ever seen a fairy kitten?"

"No, but I would love to," said John, excitedly. "Where are they kept?"

"There's plenty over there!" laughed the pixie-piper, pointing to a big pussy-willow.

John looked. He could only see a bush with soft, silvery buds growing all over it.

The pixie took up his pipe, and softly he began to play a lovely tune, looking at the pussy-willow bush all the time.

John looked too, and he saw a wonderful sight – so wonderful he could hardly believe his eyes! For the silver pussy-willow buds had changed into tiny, furry kittens, and one by one they all scrambled down the branches to the ground and ran up to the piper.

They danced and frisked round him, and ran after their little tails, for all the world like real kittens.

The piper stopped playing on his pipe.

"Now," he said, "you have to find your kitten. Which one is she? Quick! Can you see her? You must find her before they all go back to the tree and turn into pussy-willow again!"

John ran after them, and picked up a little silvery kitten small enough to fit into a nutshell! He had found his kitty!

Then he watched the others climb up the branches and one by one turn into soft, silvery buds again!

The piper blew his pipe once more, and John's kitten grew bigger and bigger until it was just the right size.

"There you are!" said the pixie. "Don't tell anyone it's a fairy kitten. They won't believe you. Thank you for helping me, and I'm glad I've been able to help you in return. Goodbye."

He vanished, and left John alone with his fairy kitten. He ran home as fast as he could.

"Why, John!" cried his mother. "So you've found your kitty after all! I am glad!"

John told heaps of people how he found his fairy kitten – but the pixie was right, nobody believed him. Not even his best friend, Robert.

He didn't mind. He knew what nobody else did – and that was the place where fairy kittens come from!

And next time you see pussy-willow, have a good look at it. I think you will say it's no wonder the fairies made kittens from such soft, furry buds!

Mr Topple and
the Egg

Mr Topple lived next door to Mr Plod the policeman. Mr Topple was a brownie, and a very nice fellow too, always ready to help anyone he could.

One day his Aunt Jemima was coming to tea, and he wanted to make a little cake for her. So he got everything ready, and then, oh dear, he found that the egg in his larder was bad.

"I must have an egg for my cake," said Mr Topple to himself. "I wonder if Mr Plod would sell me one. I'll ask him."

Mr Plod kept hens in his garden, and they laid very nice eggs. Mr Topple went to ask him, but he was out. Still, Mr Topple knew where he would be. He would be at Busy Corner, directing the traffic there.

So off he ran to Busy Corner, and told Mr Plod what he wanted. The big policeman nodded his head. "Of course you can have an egg from my hens. Run back, look in the hen-house, and take the biggest and brownest you see there."

So Mr Topple went back home. He climbed over the wall and jumped down into Mr Plod's garden. He went to the hen-house, looked round, saw one big brown egg in a nesting-box there, and came out with it in his hand.

He shut the hen-house door carefully, climbed back over the wall again, and went indoors to make his cake. He made a lovely one, and cut a big slice out of it to give to Mr Plod for his tea.

Now, as Mr Topple was climbing over the wall to get into Mr Plod's garden, little Mrs Whisper was passing by. She saw him jump down, and she watched him go into the hen-house. She saw Topple come out with an egg in his hand, and jump back over the wall into his own garden again.

"Well!" said Mrs Whisper. "Well! The nasty, horrid thief! He knows Mr Plod is down at Busy Corner, so he thought he would go over and steal an egg. Well!"

Mrs Whisper hurried on and soon she met Mr Talky. "Good morning, Mr Talky," she said. "Do you know, I've just seen the most dreadful thing – I saw Mr Topple creeping into Mr Plod's hen-house and stealing an egg! What do you think of that?"

"What a thing to do!" said Mr Talky, shocked. "I'm surprised at Mr Topple,

really I am. Dear, dear, dear – and he seems such a nice fellow too."

Mr Talky went on his way. Soon he met Miss Simple, and he stopped to speak to her. After a bit he said, "Do you know, I've just heard a most dreadful thing. I met Mrs Whisper and she told me that she saw Mr Topple creeping into Mr Plod's hen-house today and stealing an egg!"

"Well, well – would you believe it!" said Miss Simple, her eyes wide open in surprise. "You wouldn't think Mr Topple would do such a thing, would you?"

Miss Simple hurried on her way, longing to tell somebody about Mr Topple. What a bit of news! Fancy Mr Topple daring to steal an egg from the village policeman!

Miss Simple met Mrs Listen. "Mrs Listen!" she said at once, "I've just heard such a bit of news! Mr Topple – you know that nice Mr Topple the brownie, don't you? Well, do you know, he's been stealing eggs out of Mr Plod's hen-house! What do you think of that?"

"Shocking!" said Mrs Listen. "Really shocking! Something ought to be done about it!"

Off she went and soon met Mr Meddle. She told him the news. "Mr Meddle! Would you believe it, that brownie, Mr Topple, is a thief! He steals eggs. Fancy that! He was seen creeping into somebody's hen-house and stealing eggs! He's a thief. He ought to be in prison."

"So he ought, so he ought," said Mr Meddle, banging his stick on the ground. "And, what's more, I shall complain about this to Mr Plod the policeman.

Why, none of our eggs or our hens either will be safe, if Mr Topple starts stealing. There's Mr Plod over there, at Busy Corner. I'll go and tell him now."

So Mr Meddle, feeling very busy and important, went over to Mr Plod. "Mr Plod," he said, "I've a complaint to make, and I expect you to look into it. I hear that Mr Topple is a thief. I think he ought to be in prison."

Mr Plod was so surprised to hear this that he waved two lorries on at the same moment and there was nearly an accident. He stared in astonishment at Mr Meddle.

"Mr Topple a thief!" he said. "What nonsense! I've lived next door to him for years, and a kinder, more honest fellow I never met. Who says he's a thief – and what does he steal?"

"Mrs Listen told me," said Mr Meddle. "She says he steals eggs."

Mr Plod left Busy Corner and, taking Mr Meddle with him, walked off to find Mrs Listen. "What's all this about Topple stealing eggs?" he said.

"Oh," said Mrs Listen. "Well, Miss Simple told me. You'd better ask her where she got the dreadful news from. There she is, in the baker's."

Mr Plod called Miss Simple. "What's all this about Topple stealing eggs?" he said.

"Well, I heard it from Mr Talky," said Miss Simple. "He told me all about it. Dreadful, isn't it?"

"Come along," said Mr Plod to Mr Meddle, Mrs Listen and Sally Simple. "We'll all go and find Mr Talky. I'm going to get to the bottom of this."

They found Mr Talky at home. "What's all this about Topple stealing eggs?" said Mr Plod, beginning to look rather stern.

"Isn't it a shocking thing?" said Mr Talky. "I've told ever so many people and they were all surprised. It was Mrs Whisper that told me."

Mrs Whisper lived across the road. Mr Plod took them all to her house and banged on her door. She opened it, and looked surprised to see so many people outside.

"What's all this about Topple stealing eggs?" said Mr Plod.

"Oh, have you heard about it?" said

Mrs Whisper. "Well – I saw him take the egg!"

"When and where?" asked Mr Plod, taking out his notebook.

"This very morning," said Mrs Whisper. "I was passing your back garden, Mr Plod, and I happened to look over the wall – and what did I see but Mr Topple going into your hen-house, and coming out with one of your eggs in his hand – and then he jumped back over the wall again! What do you think of that? I think he ought to be in prison."

Mr Plod shut his notebook with a snap. He looked round so sternly that everyone began to feel afraid.

"This morning," said Mr Plod, in a loud, angry voice, "this morning, my friend Mr Topple came to me at Busy Corner, and said his aunt was coming to tea, and he was making her a cake. And as his egg was bad, could he have one of mine?"

There was a silence. No one dared say anything. Mr Plod went on. "I said of course he could, and so, I suppose, he

went back, and got the egg. And now, all round the town, there are people saying that Topple is a thief – a kind, honest fellow like Topple."

"I'm sure I'm sorry I said such a thing," began Mr Talky, "but I believed Mrs Whisper when she told me."

"Don't make excuses," said Mr Plod, in a thundery sort of voice. "It's all of *you* who ought to be in prison, not poor Mr Topple! How dare you say a man is a thief, Mrs Whisper, when you don't know at all whether he is or not?

"How dare you, Mr Talky, and all you others too, repeat this wicked story, when you don't know at all whether it is true or not?"

Miss Simple began to cry. "Now, one more word of this kind from any of you, and I'll be after you!" said Mr Plod. "You will all go round and tell everyone that you've made a sad mistake, and are ashamed of yourselves. Go now – for I've a very good mind to put you all in prison!"

Miss Simple gave a scream and ran

away. The others ran too, because Mr Plod looked so stern.

"I just won't have people taking somebody's good name away!" said the policeman, and he stamped back to Busy Corner. "I just won't. It's as wicked a thing as stealing!"

Well, so it is, isn't it? I think Mrs Whisper and the others will be very careful in future, don't you?

The Adventures
of the Toy Ship

Mary and Timothy had a little ship. It had fine blue sails, and its name, *Lucy Ann,* was painted on the side. The children often took it down to the stream to sail it, and it floated beautifully. It didn't turn over on its side as so many toy boats do – it sailed upright, just like a proper boat.

One day when Mary and Timothy were sailing the *Lucy Ann*, the string broke.

Oh dear! Down the stream it floated, faster and faster, and the children ran after it. But the little boat kept to the middle of the stream and, no matter how they tried, the children could not reach it.

At last they could no longer run by the stream, for someone's big garden ran right down to the edge of the water, and a fence stood in their way. Very sad, the children watched as the *Lucy Ann* disappeared around a bend in the stream. They went back home, afraid that their ship would feel very lost without them.

It did. The little ship tried its hardest to go back, but the stream took it along too fast. On and on it went until at last it came to rest beside a mossy bank. Its prow stuck into the soft earth and there it stayed. The little ship could move neither backwards nor forwards.

Night came and the little ship was

astonished to see the moon in the sky, for before it had always spent the night in the toy-cupboard.

It did not know that there were such things as moon or stars. It stared up at the big silver moon and thought it was very beautiful.

Then, suddenly, through the silence of the night there came the sound of singing. On the opposite side of the stream the little ship was surprised to see a great many twinkling lights, like tiny Japanese lanterns, shining in rainbow colours through the darkness.

It heard a lot of little voices, and saw a great number of fairy folk, all most excited. They were dressed in beautiful costumes – rose-petal waistcoats edged with diamond dewdrops, daffodil skirts and bluebell waistcoats.

Then, as the little boat watched in amazement, a ring of toadstools sprang up, and the pixies laid little white cloths on them for tables. They set out plates and glasses, and tiny knives and forks. Then they put out some tiny golden

chairs for a group of pixies who carried musical instruments.

These must be the fairy folk that Mary and Timothy sometimes talked about, thought the ship to itself. Then it saw a small boat, smaller than itself, on the opposite side of the stream, and a pixie-man got into it.

Quite nearby, on the top of its own mossy bank, the ship saw more fairy folk. They had with them all sorts of good things to eat! Honey cakes, flower biscuits, blue jellies with pink ice cream on the top, lemonade made of dew, special blancmanges in the shape of birds and animals, and many other good things.

They carried these goodies in woven baskets and on silver dishes. They were waiting for the other little boat to fetch them across the stream, so that they might lay out their food on the ring of toadstool tables.

"Hey! Little boat, come and fetch us!" they cried to the boat on the other side. The pixie-man in it began to row across. But suddenly a great fish popped up its head and made such a large wave that the pixie boat was filled with water and sank!

Oh, what a noise there was! How all the little folk shouted and cried in fear, when they saw their boat sink, and the pixie-man in the water!

"Oh, no! The boat's sunk! Oh, look at

the boatman, is he safe? Oh, what shall
we do now? We haven't another boat and
all our lovely food is on the other side of
the stream!"

Listening in dismay, the *Lucy Ann*
suddenly had a grand idea! It could take
the pixies to the other side, with all their
baskets and dishes! So it spoke up in its
funny, watery voice. How all the fairy
folk jumped when they heard it! One
little pixie was so surprised that she
dropped the dish she was carrying, and
spilled blue jelly all over the grass.

"I will take you across the stream, if

you know how to sail me," said the little ship. "Don't be frightened. I am only a toy ship, I cannot hurt you. I will be only too glad to be of help."

The pixies ran to the little ship and chattered at the tops of their silvery voices. Yes, it would do beautifully! What luck that it happened to be there! If it hadn't, the party would have been spoilt – and the King and Queen themselves were coming!

Soon the pixies had loaded all their food on board and settled down. One of them sat at the front and guided the ship out into the moonlit stream.

How proud the little toy ship was! Never before had it had anything but dolls aboard, and they couldn't do anything but sit still and stare at the sky. But these little fairy folk chattered and laughed. They ran here and there across its decks, they leaned over the side and tried to dip their fingers in the water. It was great fun for the little ship!

Out it went over the stream, sailing most beautifully. The wind filled its sails and it floated like a swan, proud and handsome.

The fairies on the other side cried out in delight – they were so grateful that the *Lucy Ann* had saved their party. And would you believe it, at that very moment the King and Queen of Fairyland arrived, riding in their golden carriage!

They watched the little boat too, and how pleased they were to see it come safely to the bank. All the fairies cheered, and the ship's blue sail trembled with joy.

The *Lucy Ann* stayed by the bank to watch the party. It smiled to see the little folk dancing to their pixie music. And then the King and Queen asked the little ship if it would take them for a sail up the stream in the moonlight. What an honour!

"Oh, Your Majesties, I would love to," said the ship. "But the stream is so

strong that I find it difficult to sail against it."

"We will help you by a magic spell," said the King. "You shall take us far up the stream, to the place where the flowers grow, and when we are tired of sailing, our butterfly carriage will bring us home. Ho there, pixies, bid our carriage follow us up the stream!"

The King and Queen stepped into the boat and off it went, sailing easily against the current, for the King had used his magic to help the ship.

How enjoyable it was, sailing along in the moonlight! The little ship had never felt so happy or so proud – after all, it was carrying the King and Queen of Fairyland.

It was a beautiful night. On either side, the banks were lined with trees that shone silver in the moonlight, and the little waves on the stream looked like silver, too.

Bats fluttered silently overhead and the old owl hooted to them as he flew by. All around them the little ship fancied it could hear the sound of fairy voices, singing a gentle lullaby. It was a most exciting journey.

After a lovely long sail the King spoke to the little ship once more.

"We will land now," he said. "Draw in to the bank, little ship. See where our butterfly carriage awaits us!"

The ship saw a beautiful carriage drawn by four yellow butterflies. It was waiting by a fence on the bank, overhung with beautiful roses.

The *Lucy Ann* sailed to the side and waited there while the King and Queen got out. Then, as it looked about, the little ship gave a glad cry.

"Why! This is where Mary and Timothy played with me this morning!" it said. "If only I could stay here, then they might find me in the morning!"

"Of course you shall stay here," said the King. "I will tie you to a stick."

So he tied the little ship tightly to a twig in the bank. The King then said goodbye and thanked the ship very much for all its help.

"I will turn your sail into a silver one, in reward for your kindness," said the Queen. In a second the ship's blue sail became one of glittering silver thread. It was really splendid. Then the King and Queen mounted their butterfly carriage and off they rode in the moonlight.

Soon it was dawn. The ship slept for a little while, and then woke up. It was proud of its glittering silver sail, and it longed for Mary and Timothy to come down to the stream to see it.

The children came running down before breakfast – and how they stared when they saw the little toy ship!

"Look at that beautiful ship!" cried Mary. "Where did it come from? It's just like ours, only it has a silver sail!"

"I wonder who tied it to that stick," said Timothy, puzzled. "Nobody comes down here but us."

"Ooh, look, Timothy – it *is* our ship! It's called *Lucy Ann*!" cried Mary, in excitement. "See, its name is on the side so it must be ours. But how did it get its beautiful sail, and who tied it up here for us to find?"

"The fairies must have had a hand in it," said Timothy. "And see, Mary – this proves it! Look at those two tiny cakes on the deck there! The fairies used our ship last night, and one of them dropped those cakes! Did you ever see such tiny things! Shall we eat them?"

"Yes – but let's save them till tonight, then maybe we'll see the fairies too!" cried Mary.

They took their ship from the water

and ran to tell their mother all about it. She was so surprised to see its silver sail!

The ship was glad to be back in the toy-cupboard. And how it enjoyed itself telling all the other toys of its adventures!

Mary and Timothy are going to eat those pixie cakes tonight. I do wonder what will happen, don't you?

The
Angry Toys

"Eileen!" said her mother. "I want you to look through your toy-cupboard and see what toys you can give away to the children in the hospital this Christmas, and to the children's home."

"Oh, Mummy – I can't bear to give any of my toys away," said Eileen.

"Don't be selfish," said her mother. "You have more toys than any other child in this town! Why, your cupboard is so full that they tumble out when you open the door!"

It was true that Eileen had a great many toys. She was lucky because she had seven uncles and five aunts, and they all gave her presents. She went to her toy-cupboard and opened the door. A box of bricks fell out and a little toy dog.

"I can't give my nice toys away," said Eileen. "I won't give my big dolls away – or even my little dolls. I won't give away my little doll's-house, even though I have a much bigger one now. I like having two."

She looked at all her toy animals. She had so many! Some of them she hadn't even given a name to, and she didn't really love any of them.

"I don't want to give away any of my large family of animals," she thought.

"They wouldn't like to be given away. They like to be together. Well – I really don't know what I can give."

At last she put a broken doll's chair and two torn books on one side to give away. That was all. Then it was time to go to bed.

When the house was quiet, the toys spoke to one another. "Did you ever know such a selfish child? Here we are, lots and lots of us, far too many for her to play with – and yet all she thinks she can spare is a broken chair and two spoiled books."

"I don't like belonging to a little girl like that," said the teddy bear. "I always wished I could belong to a nice kind little girl, who would let other children play with me sometimes. But Eileen is very selfish – she hides all her best toys when other boys and girls come to tea."

"I think she loves me and the old monkey best of all," said a big curly-haired doll, with a sweet smile and merry blue eyes. "But we don't love her, though we would like to. How can we love a little girl like that?"

"I'm not going to stay with her," said the teddy bear, suddenly. "I'm not! I know a poor little girl who would really love me. I shall go and live with her."

"And I won't stay either," said the clown. "I shall walk to the hospital, where lots of little sick children are. How they will love me! I won't stay with Eileen."

"I shall go the hospital too," said the big rocking-horse, suddenly. "I know the children who are just getting well again would like to have a ride on me."

"Let's all go," said the big doll. "Why should we stay with a little girl who isn't even generous enough to give one of her many toy animals away – why, she doesn't even know half of them! There's a toy dog at the back of the cupboard that she hasn't played with since she was given him."

"Let's go now," said the bear. So they all marched quietly out of the playroom, out of the garden door, and into the garden. Even the skittles went too.

First they went to the hospital. They had to wait till a nurse opened a door and came in – then half the toys slipped in! It was dark and quiet. They hurried into a great big room where many little children were asleep. There was a nurse at the far end of the big room, reading. She didn't see them at all. The rocking-horse stood behind a screen. The other toys sat down or lay down.

"We will wait till morning," they said. Those toys that had not gone into the hospital made their way down to the children's home. They slipped inside and

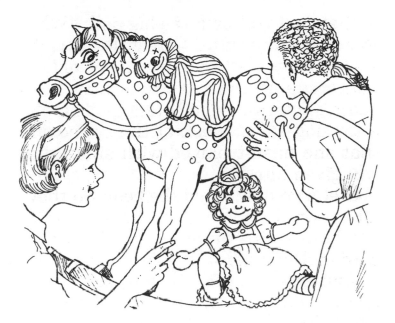

hurried off to different rooms to find new owners. Soon they had all found new homes.

How pleased and surprised the nurses in the hospital were when they suddenly found all the lovely toys! "How did they get here?" they cried. "Oh, how glad the children will be to see them!"

The children in the children's home were also delighted to wake up and find a furry rabbit or doll or toy dog cuddled up to them. They had so few toys that one nice one seemed wonderful to them.

Eileen went into her playroom the next morning and stopped to stare round in great surprise. Where were her toys? Only her books were there, and some bricks, and one or two other little things. No dolls, no teddy bear or clown, no toy animals or skittles – wherever had they all gone?

"Mummy! Mummy! My toys aren't here!" cried Eileen. "What have you done with them?"

"Nothing," said Mother, in surprise. "Well – how strange that they've all gone!"

"But where have they gone?" said Eileen, beginning to cry. "Oh, Mummy – even my curly-haired doll and my old monkey that I really did love have gone!"

"They must have walked out by themselves," said Mother, looking serious. "I expect they were disgusted with you when you wouldn't spare any of them to give away this Christmas. You knew you would have lots of new presents. You could easily have given a few away to children who have none."

"But where have they gone?" sobbed Eileen. "I want them to come back."

But they didn't come back. They are happy at the hospital, and in the children's home, because they are really loved there. Eileen still can't think where they all went to.

So if you know her, you can tell her. Won't she be surprised?

Brown Bear
has a Birthday

Once there was a brown teddy bear called Ben. For a long time he lived on a shelf in a toyshop.

Then one day a little girl bought him. She took him home and showed him to all her other toys.

"Look!" she said. "Here is a new friend for you, toys – a bear called Ben. Isn't he lovely! He's soft to cuddle – and just listen to the noise he makes when I press his middle."

"Ooooomph!" said Ben the Brown Bear, when Sarah pressed him hard in the middle. He felt very proud when Sarah spoke of him like that.

Sarah loved her new bear. She took him to bed with her at night, and the rag-doll didn't like that, because she had always been the one to go to bed with Sarah.

Ben was proud of his growl. But the toys got very tired of it. "Oooomph! Ooooomph! Ooooomph!" They heard the noise all night long when they got up to play.

"Stop making that noise," said the rag-doll. "I'm tired of it. Go and creep back into Sarah's bed. You oughtn't to leave her if she takes you to bed at night."

"I like playing with all of you," said Ben, and he pressed his middle again. "Ooooomph! I don't leave Sarah until she's asleep, and I always creep back before the morning. Ooooomph!"

Sarah gave Ben a blue ribbon to tie round his neck. He was very pleased. He sat in front of a mirror and looked at himself.

"I am a very good-looking bear, aren't I?" he said to the pink cat. She had been cleaning her fur, and she thought the bear was silly and vain. Everyone knew that the pink cat was the prettiest of all the toys. Ben thought too much of himself!

"I don't think you're at all good-looking," said the pink cat. "Your nose is too stubby, you're too fat, and I am tired of your ooooomphing."

"You're horrible," said the bear, and turned his back on the cat.

He walked away and trod on the tail of the clockwork mouse.

"Oh – you've hurt my tail!" said the little mouse. "Say you're sorry."

"Shan't!" said Ben, and he didn't.

"You haven't any manners," said the clockwork mouse. "I shall go and tell the rag-doll about you."

"Tell-tale!" said Ben, and he trod on the mouse's tail again. The mouse squealed and tried to run over to the rag-doll to tell her about Ben. But he couldn't because Ben wouldn't get off his tail.

Nobody felt very pleased with the bear after that. They wouldn't play catch or hide-and-seek with him. They wouldn't help him to untie his blue ribbon when it got into a knot.

Ben felt very sad. He went to the oldest toy, the wise old rocking-horse, whose long tail had once been chewed by Sarah's dog. It looked very sad. But

Rocking-Horse was very clever, and the toys always went to him when they were in trouble.

"Rocking-Horse, the toys are horrid to me," said Ben. "It makes me sad."

"Perhaps you've been nasty to them," said Rocking-Horse, swinging his chewed tail.

"I'm not – not really, anyway," said Ben. "I'd like to be nice to them, really I would. But they tell me I am horrid, and they won't let me play with them."

"Well, you be very, very nice to them and see what happens," said Rocking-Horse. "Now, listen to me – you've got a birthday coming soon, haven't you?"

"Yes," said Ben. "So I have. I'd quite forgotten it!"

"Well, now, you give a lovely party to the toys," said Rocking-Horse. "Give them a lovely meal, and plan lots of games, and you'll soon see they will forget you were ever nasty."

"That's a very good idea," said Ben. "I will give a party! I'll think about it hard." So he did. But he wasn't used to giving parties, and he wondered how to do it.

"I must look in my money-box and see if I have any money there," he said to himself. "If I have, I can buy some cakes and sweets and lemonade."

But there wasn't anything at all in his money-box, which wasn't surprising, because Ben had never put anything into it. He was sad.

"Now what shall I do?" he thought. "I

really must have a party. I know! I will creep into the toy sweet-shop when nobody is looking, and take some little bags of sweets. They will do nicely for the party." Now this was very naughty of him, because they were not his sweets to take. But he didn't think of that. He only thought of his party.

One night, when the toys had all gone into the toy-cupboard to have a rest after a game of hide-and-seek, Ben crept over to the toy sweet-shop. It was a lovely place. There were tiny bottles of sweets, very small bars of chocolate, some little scales for weighing, and lots of paper bags to put the sweets in.

"I'll take a bag of boiled sweets," thought Ben, and he emptied some sweets out of one of the bottles into a bag. Then he took down another bottle. It was full of tiny, round chocolates. Ben tasted one to see if it was good.

Then he got a dreadful shock! Someone popped up from behind the little counter and caught him by the shoulder!

"You bad bear! You're stealing my

sweets!" cried an angry voice.

Ben saw that the little sweet-shop doll was glaring at him, looking very cross.

"I wasn't stealing them! They were for my party! Everyone was going to have some," said Ben.

But the sweet-shop doll wouldn't believe him. He called to the other toys. "Come and see this bad bear. I caught him stealing sweets, and eating them, too! And all he says is that he was taking them for a party!"

"Party? What party? We've not heard of any party!" cried the toys.

Ben threw down the bags of sweets and went away with tears in his little button eyes. Nobody believed him. They thought he was a bad bear. What a pity! If only he could have a lovely party and make everyone happy, the toys would be nice to him again.

"I wonder if there are any cakes in the dolls' kitchen," he thought, later on. "I am sure I smelled something cooking earlier. I expect the dolls had a baking day, and baked some cakes in their little oven. I might ask them for some and put them away for my party."

So he went over to ask them. But when he arrived, the kitchen was empty. The dolls were all out paying a visit to the skittles. Ben pushed open the door and went in. He called out softly: "Is anybody here?" But nobody answered, because there was nobody there.

Ben went into the little kitchen. It was a lovely kitchen. The shelves were full of shiny pots and pans.

He opened the cupboard at the back of the kitchen and there he saw a whole plate of tiny cakes, freshly baked!

"Good!" said Ben. "I will have these for my party. I will tell the dolls when I see them. I am sure they will let me have them for my party."

He was just leaving with the plate full of cakes when three of the dolls came back from visiting the skittles.

When they saw Ben coming out with their plate of cakes they were very, very cross indeed.

"Look at this naughty teddy bear!" they cried. "First he tried to take the sweets and now he takes our cakes!" And

they told him off very severely and wouldn't listen to a word he said. None of the toys would speak to him after that, and he was very unhappy.

"I tried to do my best to have a party, but it's no good, the toys are even more unfriendly than ever!" he told the rocking-horse. "I shall run away."

"No, don't do that," said the rocking-horse. "It is a great mistake to run away from things. You set about having your party in the wrong way, you know. You should have asked the others to help you."

"I won't ask a single one of them to help me, ever!" said the bear, and he looked so angry that the rocking-horse knew it was no good talking to him any more.

The other toys came to the rocking-horse, too, and told him about the bear.

"We can't think why he is so unfriendly," they said. "He looks quite a friendly bear. But he behaves so badly."

"He's a very young bear," said the rocking-horse. "He does things the wrong

way. He wanted to be nice to you, really. What about being nice to him?"

"Oh, no. He doesn't deserve it," said Rag-Doll.

"But it would be worth it if it makes him nice and friendly again," said Rocking-Horse. "It is bad to make yourselves into enemies when you could be friends."

"Well – how could we be nice to him?" said the pink cat.

"It's his birthday next week," said Rocking-Horse. "What about giving him a party? He would love that, and so would you."

Now, somehow, that seemed a very good idea to the toys. They loved a party and, after all, if it was Ben the Brown

Bear's birthday, he ought to have a party.

"We'll give him one," said the rag-doll. "Yes, we really will!" So all the toys began to plan a fine party. But they thought they wouldn't tell the bear. It was to be a birthday surprise for him.

They went into corners and talked about it. They were always whispering together. Ben couldn't think what their secret was.

"They are saying horrible things about me!" he thought. "I shall run away. Yes, I really shall, I won't stay in this nasty place."

But the toys were only planning his party. The sweet-shop doll said he would give twelve of each of his little sweets and chocolates for the party.

"Oh, good!" said the pink cat. "That will be lovely. We all like your sweets."

"And we will bake some cakes," said the dolls. "We will make a big birthday cake, too, with three candles on. And we will make some jam tarts. You all like those."

"I'll make some lemonade," said the rag-doll.

"Hurray!" said the clockwork mouse, "that's my favourite."

"We won't make the cakes or jam tarts till the day of the birthday," said the dolls. "They will be nice and fresh then."

"We'd better give the bear some presents," said the clockwork mouse. "I could give him that blue button I found on the floor the other day."

"And I could give him my red ball," said the pink cat. "I like it very much; so I expect Ben would like it, too."

"Oh, he would," said the rag-doll. "It would be a lovely present. I think I'll make him some striped trousers from that material I've been saving for something special."

"Ben would look lovely in trousers," said the curly-haired doll. "I shall give him a bright sash to go round his waist, to keep his trousers up."

Clockwork Clown couldn't think of anything at all to give him.

"I know," he said. "I'll paint him a most beautiful birthday card," he said. "He must have a birthday card. Everybody does on a birthday."

Now, with all these exciting secrets going on, Ben grew more and more puzzled and sad.

Why wouldn't anyone tell him the secrets? Even Rocking-Horse said nothing about them. Ben went into a corner and thought hard.

"Perhaps I am a horrid little bear," he said to himself. "I expect I am vain. And I shouldn't have gone about pressing my middle and growling all the time. I won't ooooomph any more. And – oh dear – I shouldn't have taken the sweets and cakes without asking!"

The more he thought about things, the worse he felt. At last he made up his mind that he was so horrid he really should go away. He felt sure nobody would like him any more.

"I'll creep away on my birthday," he thought. "I won't tell anyone I am going. I'll put on my hat and go."

Well, when his birthday came, there was great excitement, because all the toys were getting ready for the party! Little table and chairs were set out everywhere, and cups and plates and dishes were put on them.

A delicious smell came from the dolls' kitchen, because lots of cakes and jam tarts had been made – and a most beautiful birthday cake with two candles on it!

The lemonade was in a big jug. Little dishes of sweets were on the table. The toys were dressing up in fancy dress and getting more and more excited.

"They're having a party, and they didn't tell me anything about it," thought the bear sadly, and he went and fetched his hat. "I shall go now, while they are getting ready for it."

Now, just as he was walking out of the door the clockwork clown called to him.

"Hey, Ben! Where are you going?" he said.

"I'm running away. I'm a horrid little bear, and nobody here will ever like me," said Ben. "But I'm sorry I was horrid. Goodbye, Clockwork Clown."

"Wait! Wait!" cried Clockwork Clown, and he ran over to Ben with the birthday card he had painted for him. "Many happy returns of the day, Ben! Here's a

birthday card for you!"

"Oh – how nice of you!" said Ben, and he looked at the lovely card. "Thank you. Well, goodbye. I hope you enjoy your party."

The other toys came running up, all looking very smart. "Ben! It's *your* party, silly! It's for you. Many happy returns of the day, and do please come to your own birthday party!"

Well! Ben could hardly believe his ears. His very own birthday party!

"I don't understand," he said. "How can it be mine?"

"It was a secret! We planned it for you!" said the pink cat. "Here's my present for you – a red ball to play with."

"Oh, thank you! How lovely!" said the bear. He began to feel tremendously happy. "I do wish I'd got some party clothes on, too. You all look so nice."

"Well, put some on," said the rag-doll, and gave him the new striped trousers. "These are for you."

"And you can tie this round your waist," said the curly-haired doll, and gave him the lovely sash.

Ben put on the striped trousers and the sash. They did look smart!

The clockwork mouse gave him the blue button he had found, and the curly-haired doll sewed it on the front of his trousers. Ben looked at himself in the mirror. He thought he looked very grand indeed – but he didn't say so! He let the others say it for him!

"You look so smart, Ben! You look wonderful!" they cried. "The trousers fit you well."

"And now let's have the party," said Rocking-Horse as the dolls came out carrying plates of biscuits and tarts – and a big plate with the birthday cake on!

"Many happy returns of the day!" they cried, and Ben felt happier than ever. How nice everyone was! How could he ever have thought they were horrible?

They sat down to the party. The biscuits were delicious. The jam tarts were lovely. The sweets were the nicest Ben had ever eaten. The lemonade was very tasty. All the toys drank to Ben's health. Then they cut the birthday cake. Ben had to cut the first slice, because it was his birthday. After that the clockwork clown helped him, because there were so many slices to cut.

"Wish when you take the first bite!" cried the curly-haired doll. "You always have to do that with birthday cakes!"

So everyone wished.

Then the toys cleared away the tea things, the chairs and tables were set aside, and the party games began. They played hide-and-seek and hunt-the-thimble, and then a lively game of musical chairs.

Everyone was happy and sleepy when the party was over. They climbed into the toy-cupboard to go to sleep – all except Ben, who crept, as usual, into Sarah's bed!

"Where have you been, Ben?" said Sarah, waking up.

"Ooooomph!" said Ben, sleepily. "To my birthday party. I've had a lovely time. And I do think the toys are the very nicest in all the world. I shall never, never run away from them!"

"Your birthday party!" said Sarah. "I must be asleep and dreaming!" But she knew she hadn't been asleep when, next morning, she saw Ben the Brown Bear still dressed in his party clothes! It was quite true, wasn't it? He had been to his party – and what a lovely one it was!

The
Annoying Clock

All the toys were pleased when the clock first came to live in Pat's playroom. It was a nice looking clock with a clear round face and it had four feet.

And when I say feet, I really mean feet. Instead of four little flat or round knobs that most clocks have for feet, this clock had proper shaped feet with little shoes on!

Pat was delighted with it. "Oh, Mummy – I've never seen a clock with feet before!" she said. "It does look comical. I like them. The clock has a cheeky look, somehow, as if it would quite like to take a hop, skip and a jump!"

Pat was quite right. The clock not only looked cheeky, it was cheeky! That night the toys, who were playing quietly together in a corner, heard a tap-tap-tapping upon the mantelpiece – and there was that clock doing a little tap-dance, as merry as you please!

Up and down the mantelpiece he went, tap-tap-tapping, crossing his feet in front, crossing his feet behind, grinning all over his cheeky face.

"Be careful where you're going," said the money-box pig, who also lived up on the mantelpiece.

"Don't keep bumping into us," said the bluebells in the little vase there. "You've broken one of our heads off already."

"Well, keep them out of my way then," said the clock, tapping away with his clever feet. "Hey-jig-a-jig-jig, I don't care a fig, for the money-box pig." *Bump!*

And into the pig he went again, on purpose. Then he kicked a silver thimble right off the mantelpiece. It fell down on to the fender and made the monkey jump.

"You shouldn't have done that," said the pig. "It belongs to Pat's mother."

"Well, I don't like it on my mantel-piece," said the clock. "Be careful how you talk to me, Pig. I might not like money-box pigs on my mantelpiece either!"

"It isn't your mantelpiece," said the monkey from down below. "If it belongs to anyone, it belongs to the pig, who has been there longer than anyone."

"Who's that cheeking me?" said the clock, peering over the edge of the mantelpiece. "Oh, it's you, Monkey. Well I'll just come down and tell you what I think of you!"

And to the great amazement of the

watching toys, that clock climbed cleverly down from the mantelpiece, holding on here and there by his four feet. He jumped on to the fender and then on to the hearth-rug.

He ran at the monkey, and let off his alarm at him. *R-r-r-r-r-r-r-ring!* The monkey almost jumped out of his skin, and ran away fast.

"Ha, ha!" said the clock. "That will teach you to talk cheekily to me. Tee-hee-hee, silly mon-key!"

And he danced over the floor and trod on the tail of the clockwork mouse, who squealed loudly.

Then the clock found a ball, and kicked it all round the floor with one or other of his four feet. He kicked it right into the sailor doll's middle and bowled him over like a skittle. The clock laughed so much that it sounded as if his clockwork was running down.

"Oh my, oh my! What about a game of skittles, toys? Stand up in a row and let me kick this ball at you!"

The toys were very glad indeed when the clock had to climb up to the mantelpiece again and stand still and behave himself.

"What a pest!" said the sailor doll.

"Too many feet, that's what's the matter with him," said the monkey, gloomily.

"Can't we unscrew them?" said the cat, whose head unscrewed very cleverly, so that pencils and rubbers could be kept inside her.

"We might try," said the bear. But as

soon as the monkey climbed up to the mantelpiece to see if he could unscrew the clock's feet, the clock kicked out with his front ones and shot the monkey right off the mantelpiece!

"Oh, oh! I'm falling!" cried the monkey, and he landed right on top of the fat teddy bear. He didn't hurt himself, but he knocked all the growl out of the bear's middle, so that he could only squeak instead, which upset him very much.

"Pat will think I'm the clockwork mouse, not the teddy bear," he said gloomily. "Eeeee! There I go again. Nothing but a squeak left. What are we going to do about that annoying clock? Here he comes again!"

Laughing because he had kicked the monkey off the mantelpiece, the clock climbed down to tease the toys as usual. He danced a tap-dance on the roof of the doll's-house and scared the little dolls inside terribly, because they thought it must be raining heavily on their roof. He found the box of marbles and kicked them at all the toys till they ran to hide

in the cupboard. He really was a very good shot. He laughed so much that he had to stop.

"Oh dear, oh dear! This is fun," said the clock. "What a silly lot you are, to be sure! I shall have great fun with you every night."

The poor toys were very upset. How could they stop this tiresome clock from annoying them each night? It was quite impossible to unscrew his feet. He was too quick to catch when he was dancing round the room, and anyway they were afraid of him.

It was the clockwork mouse who thought of the Great Idea, and whispered it to the monkey.

"Take his key away! I'm sure it's his clockwork that keeps him going on his feet, as well as turns his hands round in front of his face. Take his key away!"

"Good idea!" whispered back the monkey. "I'll tell the money-box pig and get him to throw the key down to us tonight. We won't say a word to the clock."

So they sent the brown spider, who lived in a dark corner, to tell the money-box pig the Great Idea. And the pig was very glad because the night before he had almost been knocked off the mantelpiece by the tiresome clock, doing a madder dance than usual.

The pig waited till the clock began to dance. His key was always left behind him on the mantelpiece when he danced, in case it fell out. The pig waited till the clock was tap-tap-tapping at the other end of the mantelpiece, and then he quickly clattered over to the key on his four stiff china legs. He thrust against the key with his snout, and it went flying over the edge. *Clang!* It hit the fender and jumped to the hearth-rug.

Quick as lightning the monkey pounced on it and ran off with it. He went to the jigsaw-puzzle box, opened the lid, and put the key in among all the pieces there.

The clock heard the clang and wondered what it was that had fallen. When he saw that his key was missing, he was horrified. Down he climbed to the floor at once.

"My key fell off!" he cried to the toys. "Help me to look for it. I can't go unless I'm wound up."

"Don't want to look for it," said the monkey, the bear, the sailor doll and the mouse. And they wouldn't. Anyway, they knew where it was, and they giggled to see the clock turning up the edge of the hearth-rug with his feet, and hunting in the coal-scuttle for his key.

Well, of course, he didn't find it and he was so long in looking for it that his clockwork ran down and he stopped. He lay on the hearth-rug not ticking at all. Not even a foot waggled.

"Aha! Peace at last!" said the bear. "Serves him right!"

Pat found him there in the morning and was puzzled to know how her clock came to be on the hearth-rug. She put him back on the mantelpiece and felt for the key. But it wasn't there. Pat hunted for it, but she couldn't find it.

"Well, you're not much use without a key," she told the clock. "I'll keep you for a while to see if I find the key, but if I don't you'll have to be thrown away."

The clock was very upset. The monkey told him that the toys had taken his key, and were going to keep it. But they were sorry to think he might be thrown away, so one night the monkey fetched it from the jigsaw box and gave it back to him.

"Now, I'll wind you up just this once," said the monkey. "If you behave, we'll leave the key with you: if you don't, we shall hide it again. See?"

Well, the clock behaved beautifully, and didn't come down from the mantelpiece at all. He did one little dance, but when he bumped into the money-box pig he said he was very sorry, so the toys felt sure he was going to turn over a new leaf. All the same, I would like to see him tap-tap-tapping on his four little feet, wouldn't you?

A Visit to
a Wizard

Now once a very strange thing happened to Tom Toots. He was going through Ho-Ho Wood when he came to a small cottage he was sure he had never seen before.

"Funny!" said Tom Toots, stopping. "That wasn't here when I last came this way – and yet it's an old cottage, so it must have been there!"

He noticed that smoke was coming from the chimney, and then he really did stare. It was green smoke – and everyone knows what that meant! Green smoke only comes from the chimneys of houses belonging to witches or wizards!

"Well, well, well – who'd have thought I'd ever see green smoke!" thought Tom, and he went very quietly to the cottage. Maybe he could peep through a window and see something exciting.

He walked round the cottage and came to a window. There didn't seem to be a door anywhere! So he looked through the window.

He saw a very strange thing. A wizard stood in the middle of a chalk circle, drawn on the floor. He had his eyes shut and his arms outspread, and he was muttering magic words. Tom couldn't hear what they were.

And suddenly the wizard shrank and shrank until he was as small as a doll –

and there he stood, dancing about in glee in the middle of the ring! Tom's eyes nearly fell out of his head! He pressed his nose against the window to see better – and the wizard saw him. Quickly, he muttered more magic words, and hey presto, he shot up to his own size again – but he went on growing till his head bumped against the ceiling! Tom was quite scared. Would the wizard's head go through it?

The wizard felt the ceiling pressing against his head, and shouted out a very magic word indeed – and went back to his proper size. He grinned at Tom and shouted to him.

"That was just a little mistake!" he said. "I'm not very good at that spell yet. Come on in!"

"I can't find the door!" said Tom, excited.

"Oh sorry – I forgot about the door," said the wizard, and took up a glittering wand. He waved it.

"Icckly-ockly-oogly-PFFFFFF!" he yelled – and a door appeared in the wall

by the window. Tom was so surprised
that he stared at the door instead of
opening it.

"Come in, come in, come in!" called
the wizard. "Don't you know how to open
a door?"

Tom went in. The wizard nodded at
him. "Shut the door. There's an awful
draught," he said. "I'm glad to see you. I
want a bit of help this morning."

"Well – I'm not much good at magic,"
said Tom. "But I'm willing to learn."

And then began a most exciting

morning. Tom had to watch the wizard turning himself into a bright fire burning in the middle of the floor – and when the fire began to pop like fireworks, he had to pour a jug of water over it at once.

Sizzle-sizzle-sizzle! The fire died down at once and a great billow of green smoke rose up – and turned into the wizard! He looked very pleased.

"That was good," he said. "First time I've been able to do that properly. Thanks very much. Now I want to change myself into a mouse, and see if I can get down that hole. It's a very useful thing to know how to do, because if I'm in a spot of trouble, I can change into a mouse, slip down a hole and escape from any enemy at once."

"Well, how can I help you with that?" asked Tom, delightedly.

"Would you hold my big black cat for me?" said the wizard. "You see, he might not know that the mouse was really me, his master, and he might run after me. Just hold him, will you?"

Tom saw the cat for the first time. It

was an enormous black cat with eyes as green as cucumbers. It sat on a black cushion in a corner, and Tom was quite surprised to see it there.

He picked it up and sat down with it on his knee. The cat didn't seem to mind. It began to purr so loudly that Tom thought it was imitating a motor-bike!

"My cat likes you," said the wizard, pleased. "Are you sure you don't know any magic? He usually only purrs like that with witches and wizards. Now watch – this mouse magic is very interesting. I hope I do it properly. Last time I changed into a horse by mistake, and the cat leaped out of the window in fright."

He stepped into the magic ring again and spun round very fast, his cloak flying out round him. He sang as he went, but the words were so magic and sung so fast that Tom could only make out a few.

"Cha-cha-choo ... oofle-oofle-oof ... abbididee ..."

Then, to Tom's enormous astonishment, the wizard began to grow long mouse whiskers!

He grinned at Tom as he spun. "The spell's beginning to work!" he shouted, and chanted some more magic words. In about thirty seconds he began to grow smaller and smaller, his clothes disappeared, fur grew instead, a tail appeared – and goodness me, he had turned into a small frisky mouse running all round the room!

The cat stopped purring. It stared at the mouse, astonished. It dug its claws into Tom's knee and hissed, trying to

leap off to catch the mouse, but Tom held on tight.

"Go down a hole!" he yelled to the wizard. "I can't hold this cat much longer. Go down a hole!"

The cat scratched Tom, but still he held on to it tightly – and at last the wizard-mouse found a hole and disappeared down it at top speed. Tom let the cat go then, and it ran to the hole, sniffing and mewing.

"You fierce creature!" said Tom crossly, looking at his scratched hand. "Now what am I to do? The wizard can't come out of the hole while you're sniffing at it.

I'd better open the door and shoo you out!"

So he opened the door but the cat wouldn't go out. Tom scratched his head, puzzled. How did you get a cat out into the garden if it wouldn't go? He went to a cupboard and opened it, wondering if there was any milk there so that he could pour some into a saucer, and put it down outside the door.

There wasn't any milk. But there was a plate of cooked fish!

"Ha!" said Tom, and took it. "Just what we need, Puss!"

He let the cat get a sniff of the fish and then carried the plate to the door, the cat following him at once. He set the plate down outside and the cat ran to it.

Slam! Tom shut the door and yelled loudly:

"Hey, Wizard. You can come out! I've put the cat outside!"

And out of the hole came the little mouse, scampering on four tiny paws. It ran into the magic ring, and Tom heard it squeaking loudly, as if it were saying magic words in mouse language! Then he stared in great surprise!

The mouse had suddenly disappeared – and in its place was the wizard – but oh how very very tiny! No bigger than the mouse had been!

The wizard soon grew though. It was marvellous to see him growing bigger and taller. Soon there he was, grinning at Tom, his own size again.

"Thanks very, very much," he said. "You really are a very bright boy. How did you get the cat away?"

"I gave him a plate of fish out of your cupboard," said Tom.

"What!" shouted the wizard. "Fish! That was my dinner! You silly, stupid, little—"

"Well, if I hadn't you'd still be down that hole, with the cat sniffing at it," said Tom, in alarm, for the wizard's eyes seemed to be on fire, he was so angry. "I think I was pretty clever to think of getting the cat outside like that."

"Yes – yes, you were," admitted the wizard, patting Tom and looking pleased again. "In fact, I think you are a remarkably clever boy – quite brilliant! I'll offer you a sack of gold if you'll stay here with me, and help me. What about it? I'll teach you plenty of magic tricks."

"No, thank you," said Tom. 'I can do a few tricks myself already – not as good as you do, of course – and I don't think I really want to learn magic like yours. I'd be scared I couldn't get back to my own shape if I turned myself into a mouse – or some other animal. I think I'll go now. Goodbye."

"Wait a bit, wait a bit!" said the wizard, holding his sleeve. "I like you, and I'd like to hear about the tricks you can do. And anyway, I've made the door disappear, so you can't go yet."

Sure enough, when Tom looked round, the door had gone again, and walls went all round the room!

"You let me go," said Tom fiercely. "And don't you dare use any of your magic on me. I might use some on you, for all you know!"

"Now listen – I'll make a bargain with you," said the wizard. 'You tell me one thing you can do that I can't and I'll let you go at once. Go on – tell me!"

Poor Tom! He only knew a few card tricks – two were easy card tricks that anyone could do – one was a balancing trick with glasses, and he was sure the wizard could do that. Ah, but wait a minute, wait a minute – what about that trick with one single playing-card?

"Listen," said Tom, boldly. "I think I can do something you can't do." He took a pack of playing cards from his pocket, and slid one out, putting it on the table. "Can you do any magic of any sort that will enable you to put your head right through that card, so that it hangs round your neck – *without* making yourself small?"

The wizard stared at the playing card and frowned. "No," he said. "I can't. And I don't believe anyone can, certainly not a boy like you. I don't think there's any magic for that."

"Well, I can do it without magic!" said Tom.

"Fibber!" said the wizard. "Go on – do it and if you do put your head through that card, I'll let you go – and give you a bag of money too!"

"Right!" said Tom. "Can you give me a pair of sharp scissors, please?"

"Here you are," said the wizard, taking a pair out of Tom's pocket, much to his surprise, for they certainly hadn't been there before!

"Now watch," said Tom, flourishing the scissors. "I hold the card so – and I fold it in half. Now I take the scissors and cut slits in it from the folded edge – see? But I don't cut them right to the other edge."

He did as he said, and the wizard watched him. "Now I turn the card round, with the two edges towards me," said Tom, "and cut more slits between the other slits I've made, see? But I stop before I get to the top, as I did before."

"This is silly," said the wizard. "This isn't putting your head through the card. It's ..."

"Be patient," said Tom. "The magic doesn't appear till I've finished! Now see – I am going to cut along the top fold – between the first slit and the last. There!" He had slipped his scissor points into the fold without cutting the first little piece, and had cut along the fold to the last slit, but not the end of the fold. Then he slipped the scissors out and put them on the table. This is what the playing card looked like now, when he unfolded it very gently.

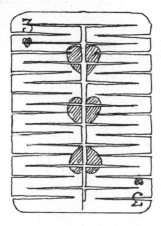

The wizard laughed. "Well, what about this wonderful way of putting your head through the card? You can cut all you like – but what I want to see is how you get your head through it."

Tom opened up the card very carefully indeed – one tear and the trick wouldn't work! What a long long strip circle he had – look at it!

"I'll pop my head through now, and let it hang round my neck!" said Tom, and over his head went the slitted card, making the wizard stare in great surprise.

At first he looked angry – then he began to laugh. "It isn't magic! But it's a very good trick! Fancy, I didn't know how to do it! Well, well – I was right – you are a clever boy. Won't you please stay with me and help me?"

"No," said Tom. "Where's that bag of money, please?"

"Oh well – you deserve it," said the wizard, and took a small empty bag from the shelf. He blew into it, said a magic word in a low voice – and it suddenly grew fat and heavy. The wizard shook it and it jingled loudly.

"Catch!" he said, and threw it to Tom. The boy caught it in delight. He peeped into it – yes, it was full of gold. Whatever would his mother say?

"What about making the door come back again now?" said Tom, and the wizard poked at the wall with his wand. Hey presto, there was the door again! He caught Tom's arm as he was going out.

"Would you mind leaving me that slit card, please?" he said. "You've still got it round your neck. I'm afraid I might not remember exactly how to do the cutting, if you take it away."

Tom laughed, and took off the card necklace very carefully, so that it wouldn't be torn.

"Here you are," he said. "Puzzle your wizard friends with my trick. Fancy a wizard not knowing how to put his head through a card! Goodbye – I'm off!"

Could you have done what Tom did? You couldn't? Well, try it – it's quite easy. Then if you ever happen to meet a wizard, you'll know how to get the better of him!

Santa's Workshop

In the playroom all the toys were getting ready for Christmas. The doll's-house dolls were making paperchains, the wind-up sailor was baking mince-pies, even Panda was helping to make decorations, and he had only arrived in there three weeks before – a present from the children's Aunt Jane.

All the toys were helping, except for one – the big rocking-horse that lived in the middle of the room. He was a fine fellow with a lovely spotted coat, a big mane and a bushy black tail.

He rocked back and forth and took the children for long rides round the playroom floor. They all loved him – but the toys were afraid of him.

Sometimes he would begin to rock

when they were playing around, and then, how they ran out of the way!

Sometimes he was so proud and so vain that he would not play with the other toys.

"I'm too important to do boring things like making paperchains," he boasted. "I'm the only toy in this playroom big enough for the children to ride on. I ought to be king of the playroom for Christmas."

"Well, you don't deserve to be," said the curly-haired doll. "You squashed the monkey's tail yesterday, and that was unkind."

"I didn't mean to," said the rocking-horse, offended. "He shouldn't have left it lying around under my rockers. Silly of him."

"You should have looked down before you began to rock, and you would have seen it," said the doll.

"Well! Do you suppose I'm going to bother to look for tails and things before I begin to rock?" said the rocking-horse. "You'll just look out for yourselves!

That's the best thing to do."

But the toys were careless. Later that morning the little red toy car ran under the horse's rockers and had his paint badly scratched. Next, the wind-up sailor left his key there and the rocking-horse bent it when he rocked on it. It was difficult to wind up the sailor after that, and he was cross.

Then the curly-haired doll dropped her bead necklace and the rocking-horse rocked on it and smashed some of the beads. The toys were really upset with him about that.

"Be careful, be careful!" they cried. "Tell us before you rock, Rocking-Horse! You might rock on one of us and hurt us badly!"

But the rocking-horse just laughed and thought it was a great joke to scare the toys so much.

"You are not kind," said Ted, the big teddy bear. "One day you will be sorry."

And so he was, as you will hear.

It happened that, on the day before Christmas, Sarah and Jack had been playing with their toys and had left them all around the room when they had gone for lunch.

Now, the panda's head, and one of his ears, were just under the rocker of the rocking-horse. And as soon as the children had left the room the rocking-horse decided to rock.

"Stop, Rocking-Horse! Stop!" shrieked the toys, running forward. "Panda is underneath!"

But the rocking-horse didn't listen. No, he thought the toys were scared as usual, and he didn't listen to what they said. Back and forth he rocked – and poor Panda was underneath!

Oh dear, oh dear, when the toys got to him what a sight he was! Some of his nice black fur had come out, and his right ear was all squashed. The toys pulled him away and began to cry.

"What's the matter?" asked the rocking-horse, stopping and looking down.

"You naughty horse! We told you to stop! Now see what you have done!" cried the toys angrily. "You are really very unkind. We won't speak to you or play with you any more."

"Don't then," said the horse, and he rocked away by himself. *Cree-eek, cree-eek!* "I'm sure I don't want to talk to you or give you rides if you are going to be so cross with me."

After that the toys paid no attention to the naughty rocking-horse.

They made a great fuss over Panda, who soon stopped crying. Then they went on getting ready for Christmas. Ted wrapped up a present for the pink cat, Rag-Doll made a Christmas stocking, and Jack-in-the-Box helped the other toys hang tinsel on the Christmas tree. They had such fun!

In the corner of the room, Rocking-Horse felt sad. He usually helped hang the tinsel because he could reach higher than the other toys.

"I wish they'd talk to me!" he thought to himself. "I wish they'd play. I'd like

to give them each a ride round the playroom – in fact, I'd take three of them at once if they asked me."

But the toys acted as if the rocking-horse wasn't there at all. They didn't ask him to help with anything. They didn't even look at him.

"He's unkind and selfish and horrid," they said. "And the best way to treat people like that is not to pay any attention to them."

So the rocking-horse got sadder and sadder, and longed to gallop round the room just for a change. But he was afraid the toys might be cross if he did.

Now, just as it was getting dark the

children's puppy came into the room, because someone had left the door open. The toys fled to the toy-cupboard in fear, because the puppy was very playful and liked to carry a toy outdoors and chew it.

Everyone got safely into the cupboard except the pink cat. She slipped and fell, and the puppy pounced on her. He chewed and nibbled her whiskers clean away! Nobody dared to rescue her, not even the rocking-horse, though he did wonder if he should gallop at the puppy.

Then somebody whistled from downstairs, and the puppy flew out of the door. The poor pink cat sat up. "Oh!" she said. "Whatever has happened to my beautiful pink whiskers?"

"They've gone," said Panda, peeping out of the cupboard. "The puppy has chewed them off. There they are, look, on the floor, in tiny little bits."

The pink cat cried bitterly. She had been proud of her whiskers. "A cat doesn't look like cat without her whiskers," she wept.

The sound of the pink cat crying made

Panda feel so sad that soon he was crying too. "What shall we do?" he wailed. "Oh, what shall we do? When Sarah and Jack see us, all nibbled and squashed, they will throw us into the dustbin. Boo-hoo-hoo!"

"Yes," sobbed the pink cat. "They won't want us if they are given brand-new toys for Christmas." And before long the playroom was filled with the sound of toys crying.

How the rocking-horse wished he had not been so unkind! He would miss any of the toys terribly if they were thrown away – and it would be mostly his fault, too! Whatever could he do to earn their forgiveness? He looked round the room at all the Christmas decorations and suddenly he knew just what to do.

"Excuse me, toys – but I've got an idea," he said in his humblest voice.

"It's only the rocking-horse," said Ted. "Don't pay any attention to him."

"Please do pay some attention," said the horse. "I've got a good idea. I can take all the broken toys to Santa Claus's

workshop. I know the way because I came from there. Perhaps Santa Claus can fix you all and make you better."

"But it's Christmas Eve!" cried Panda. "Santa will be too busy delivering presents to have time for us."

"Oh no!" replied Rocking-Horse. "Santa is the friend of every old toy. No matter how busy he is, I'm sure he will find time to help us if we ask him tonight!"

"Well! Let's go then," said the teddy bear. So the toys helped Pink Cat and Panda, the wind-up sailor and the monkey, the curly-haired doll and the

little red toy car all up on to Rocking-Horse's back. Then Ted sat at the very front and said, "Let's go!"

Cree-eek, cree-eek! went Rocking-Horse, across the floor and up, away out of the window and into the night sky. For miles and miles they travelled, rocking past twinkling stars towards the great hill where Santa Claus lived.

Luckily for the toys, Santa was at home. He was busy piling a new load of presents on to his magic sleigh. His faithful reindeer would take them fast and far – to the other side of the world in the blink of an eye. When he heard the sound of the rocking-horse neighing and hrrumphing at the door, he came to see who was there.

Rocking-Horse explained why they had come and, to the toys' delight, Santa said he would be glad to help. He only had three more loads to deliver before morning. Then he inspected each of the toys in turn to see what the damage was.

"Dear, dear!" said Santa Claus, looking severely at the rocking-horse. "I hope you are ashamed of yourself. I have heard of you and your stupid ways of scaring the toys by rocking suddenly when they are near. Come in!"

The horse rocked in and followed Santa Claus to his workshop. In no time at all Santa had straightened out the wind-up sailor's key and mended the curly-haired doll's broken beads. He soon fixed the monkey's squashed tail and patched up the toy car's scratched paint.

Then it was Panda's turn. Santa opened a drawer and looked into it.

"Dear me!" he said. "I've no panda fur left. It's all been used up. Now what am I to do?" He turned and looked at the rocking-horse.

"You've a nice thick black mane!" he said. "I think you'll have to spare a little for Panda!"

Then, to the rocking-horse's horror, he took out a pair of scissors and cut off a piece of his thick mane! How strange it looked!

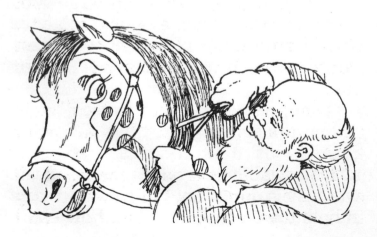

Quickly and neatly, Santa Claus put the black fur on to the panda's head. He stuck it there with glue, and it soon dried. Then Santa looked at Panda's squashed ear.

He found a new ear and carefully put it on. It belonged to a teddy bear, really, so it was brown instead of black, and looked rather odd.

"Now, I've no special black paint!" said Santa in a vexed tone. "Only blue or red. That won't do for a panda's ear. Ha, I'll have to take off one of your nice black spots, Rocking-Horse, and use it for the panda's ear. That will do nicely!"

He carefully scraped off a large spot from the rocking-horse's back, mixed it with a tiny drop of water and then painted it on Panda's new ear. It looked fine!

"Thank you very much indeed!" said the panda, gratefully. "You are very kind."

"Not at all!" said Santa, beaming all over his big, kind face. "I'm always ready to help toys, you know! And how can I help you?" he said, looking at the pink cat. She soon explained all about her whiskers.

"Oh dear, oh dear, oh dear!" said Santa shaking his head sadly. "I'm right out of whiskers."

Just then, a small voice piped up behind him. It was Rocking-Horse.

"I should be very pleased to give the toy cat some of the hairs out of my long black tail," he said. "They would do beautifully for whiskers."

"But how can we get them out?" said the pink cat.

"Pull them out, of course," said the rocking-horse.

"But it will hurt you," said the pink cat.

"I don't mind," said the rocking-horse, bravely. "Pull as many as you like!" So Santa pulled eight out, and it did hurt, but the horse didn't make a sound.

Then Santa carefully gave the cat her whiskers back. "One whisker!" he said. "Two whiskers! Three whiskers! Oh, you will look fine when I have finished, Pink

Cat. These are black whiskers, long and strong, and you will look very handsome now." And so she did. Very fine indeed!

At last it was time to go, so all the toys clambered back on to the rocking-horse.

"Thank you, Santa," they cried as they left. "Thank you for helping us all."

Then off they went home again, rocking hard all the way in order to get home by morning, and glad to be good as new again.

The toys cheered when they saw them.

"What glorious fur you have – and look at your fine new ear!" they cried when they saw Panda. "And look at your lovely whiskers," they said to Pink Cat.

Rocking-Horse said nothing. He stood in the middle of the playroom floor, quite still, not a rock left in him.

"Santa took some of Rocking-Horse's hair for me, and one of his spots to paint my ear black," said Panda. "You can see where he had a bit cut from his mane, and one of his biggest spots is missing."

Sure enough, it was just as Panda had said.

"I must say it was nice of the rocking-horse to give you them," said Ted, suddenly.

"And to give me my new whiskers," added Pink Cat. "Especially as we haven't even spoken to him lately. Very nice of him."

All the other toys thought the same. So they went over to the rocking-horse, who was still looking sad.

"Thank you for taking us to Santa's workshop," said the curly-haired doll.

"It was very kind of you," said the monkey.

"I can't thank you enough!" said the pink cat. "I had pink whiskers before, and they didn't show up very well – but these show beautifully. Don't you think so?"

"You look very handsome," said the rocking-horse. "Very!"

"Your tail looks a bit thin now, I'm afraid," said the pink cat. "Do you mind?"

"Not a bit," said the rocking-horse. "I can rock back and forth just as fast when my tail is thin as when it's thick. You get on my back and see, Pink Cat!"

So up got the pink cat, and the rocking-horse went rocking round the playroom

at top speed. It was very exciting. You may be sure the rocking-horse looked where he was going this time! He wasn't going to rock over anyone's tail again!

"Oh, thank you!" said the pink cat, quite out of breath. "That was the nicest ride I ever had!"

"Anyone can have one!" said the horse, rather gruffly, because he was afraid that the toys might say "No" and turn their backs on him.

But they didn't. They all climbed up at once.

"Nice old rocking-horse!" they said. "We're friends again now, aren't we? Gallop away, gallop away!"

And you should have seen him gallop away again, round and round the room until the sun peeped through the curtains.

"Merry Christmas! Merry Christmas!" they heard the children shouting.

"Good gracious," said Ted, the big teddy bear. "It's Christmas Day!" All the toys had quite forgotten.

And a lovely Christmas Day it turned

out to be, too. Sarah and Jack were
amazed at how smart all their old toys
looked – apart from Rocking-Horse,
whose mane and tail looked a bit straggly.

"Never mind," said Sarah. "We will
always love you, toys, even if you are old
and worn, won't we, Jack?"

"Oh yes," said Jack. "Merry Christmas
toys. Merry Christmas to you all!"

Thirty-Three Candles

"I don't want Yah to come to my birthday party," said Twinks. "I don't like him."

"Oh, but we must ask him!" said Twinks's mother. "He'll be so offended if we don't. He might do all sorts of horrible things to us."

"He's a nasty, horrid, unkind goblin," wailed Twinks. "He'll spoil my party!"

"Well, he'll blow our house down, or make our hens disappear or something like that if we leave him out of the party," said Mrs Twinks. "Anyway, he'll be sure to do lots of tricks at the party – he's very good at those, just as good as a conjuror."

"I don't like him or his tricks, and I won't like my party," said poor Twinks, gloomily.

All the same, Mrs Twinks knew she had to ask Yah. He was a very powerful little goblin, and goodness knows what he would do if he wasn't asked.

The day of the party came. Mrs Twinks had made all kinds of sandwiches, cakes, biscuits and jellies. She had made a birthday cake, too, with thirty-three candles on it. Although Twinks was very small, brownies are not grown up until they are more than a hundred years old, so thirty-three was really quite young for a brownie.

Yah came with the other guests, dressed in a magnificent sparkling suit.

"It is made of flames, sewn with snippings of moonlight and then damped down a bit with mist," he said. "Nice, isn't it?"

He looked round at the tea table. "Ah – not a bad spread, Mrs Twinks. Would you like to see me eat a whole plateful of sausage rolls at one gulp?"

Mrs Twinks didn't want to see that at all, and neither did anyone else. Those lovely sausage rolls! Everyone wanted one of those! Yah beckoned with his fingers, and opened his mouth wide – and one by one the sausage rolls flew through the air and straight into his mouth! "What a waste!" whispered poor Twinks to his mother.

"Very nice," said Yah, and sat down at the table. He caught sight of the balloons hanging all around the room. "Ah – have you seen my new trick of sending sharp looks at balloons – so sharp that they burst? Ha, ha, ha!"

"You couldn't do that!" said Twinks. "Sharp looks wouldn't burst balloons!"

But they did! Every time Yah looked

sharply at a balloon it went pop! Soon there were no balloons left. Twinks was almost in tears. His mother frowned at him. She hoped he wasn't going to be rude to Yah. Oh dear – Yah was such a nuisance!

"Ah – jellies!" said Yah. "Have you ever seen jellies playing leap-frog?"

"No – and I don't want to," said Twinks, crossly. "Leave them alone!"

But, no – Yah did a bit of magic, the jellies jumped over one another, and before long there was one big mix-up of jellies in a dish, all wobbling and shivering in fright.

"They'll taste horrid," said Twinks. "Mother, stop him. He's being silly. He's not being clever! Mother, please light the candles on my cake. It's time they were lit."

"You think I'm silly, not clever, do you?" said Yah, glaring at him. "Well, then, I'll turn myself into a little flame and light every single one of your thirty-three candles!"

And before anyone could say "Please don't!" Yah had disappeared, and a tiny yellow flame appeared in the air over the big iced birthday cake. Everyone watched in amazement. Yes – that was really clever of Yah!

All round the cake went the little magic flame, lighting one candle after another.

A tiny voice called out, "Aren't I clever? I'm Yah the goblin, the cleverest in the world! I'm a burning flame. One candle, two, three – twenty-one – twenty-nine – thirty-two – now watch when I get to the last one. I'll sit on it myself, a little goblin-flame!"

And now all the candles were alight, and burning merrily. Yah's flame sat on the last candle, bigger and brighter than the others.

"Mother," said Twinks, suddenly. "Birthday candles always have to be blown out, don't they? And if I wish when I blow them out, my wish comes true, doesn't it?"

"Only if you blow them all out at once," said his mother. "I don't think anyone could blow out thirty-three candles in one blow. Don't try! Yah would be angry."

"Yes, very angry!" called the little

high-burning voice from Yah's own
flame. "Let the candles burn down and I
will blow them out!"

"But it's my cake!" shouted Twinks,
and he took an enormous breath. Then
he blew the breath out of his mouth with
a great big blow! *Whooooooooooosh!*

They're going out – half are out – some
more are going out – and now there's
only one left. Twinks only had a little of
his one big blow left – but it was enough.
The last candle went out – the one that
Yah had sat himself on as a little flame.
The candles sent tiny spires of smoke up
– they were all out! Nobody said a word.

Then Mrs Twinks spoke. "Yah! Where are you? I'm so sorry Twinks blew like that. Please don't punish him!"

There was no answer. Twinks giggled. "Mother," he said, "don't you know what's happened? I've blown Yah out too, like all the candle flames! I don't know where flames go to – but wherever it is, Yah is with them. He isn't here any more – and he'll never come back. When I blew the candles out I wished that he would vanish for ever!"

"Twinks has got rid of him!" shouted his friends, and danced round the room. "Horrid old Yah! He's gone!"

Well – Yah certainly didn't come back. It was most extraordinary. Laughing happily, the guests began to eat the birthday tea again, and how they enjoyed it without Yah there to spoil things for them. Nobody lit the candles again, though. They thought that Yah might come back again if they did!

But he never did come back, and Twinks was made a great fuss of after that.

Nemo and
the Sea-Dragon

Long, long ago there lived a good king
and queen called Teleus and Cleo. They
had a little son who was not yet a year
old, and they loved him very much.

Before the baby had celebrated his first
birthday, a great army rose up against
the king, his father. At once Teleus
marched against his enemy, but alas for
him, he was slain, and all his generals
were taken prisoners.

The prince at the head of the
conquering army at once made himself
king. He sent for his servants and bade
them take Cleo the queen and cast her
and her baby into the sea.

They searched for her, and found her
hiding in a tower with her little son.
Roughly they dragged her out and pulled

her down the steps of the tower. They took her to the seashore, and were about to throw her into the raging waters, when she knelt down before them, and begged for mercy.

"Do not drown my baby," she prayed them. "What harm has he ever done anyone? Have mercy on us, I beseech you."

"We have been bidden to cast you both into the sea," answered the men.

"Cannot you give me a boat?" begged the poor queen.

"No," said the men, and threw her and the baby into the waters. But one man, kinder than the others, saw an old wooden chest lying on the beach nearby, and he took this and cast it into the sea near to where the queen was struggling.

She managed to reach it, and put the baby safely in. Then, with much difficulty, she clambered into the chest herself. By this time the men were gone, save the one who had cast the chest into the water. He, because he had a wife and baby son at home, was sorry for the queen, and wading out into the sea some little way, he threw his bag into the chest.

The queen could give him no thanks, for she was too frightened. At the bottom of the chest were some old bits of canvas, and these she wrapped round her little son, fearful lest the drenching he had had should cause his death.

The strange boat floated on and on, tossed by the waves, while the queen ate some of the bread and meat that she

found in the bag, and tried to keep the baby warm. Presently night came and she slept.

Another day came and went, and for the second night the queen saw the stars gleaming in the sky, and wondered where the chest was floating to. There was no more food left, and the poor woman made up her mind that she and her son would soon perish.

At the dawn of the third day, the queen was awakened by a curious grating noise. She sat up and saw that the tide was flinging the chest on to a sloping, stony beach. At once she began to call loudly for help, and soon an old fisherman and his wife came running to the shore.

When the man saw the floating chest was in danger of being smashed to pieces on the stones and rocks, he waded into the water and caught hold of it. Then, with the help of his wife, he drew it to the shore, and stared in amazement at the sight of a woman and a baby in such a strange craft.

"Who are you, and from whence do you come?" he asked the wet and weary queen.

But she would tell him nothing. She was afraid that if he knew who she was, he might betray her secret for gold. She

pretended to have forgotten everything, and begged the fisherman and his wife to shelter them and give them food.

Now they were a kindly couple, and they welcomed the young woman and her son to their poor little hut. They gave them dry clothes and good food, though served in poor, mean dishes, and for many days the queen stayed with them until she had recovered from her weariness.

"I must go now," she said one day. "You have been so kind to me, but I cannot take your food for nothing any longer, I must find some work to do, and leave you."

But the fisherman's wife had grown so fond of the gentle and beautiful young woman that she could not bear to let her go. As for her husband, he thought the world of the sturdy little boy. He had no children of his own and had always longed for some.

"Look now," he said, when he heard that his visitor was going to leave them. "Why do you go? There is nowhere on

133

this desolate island for you to go to. We have grown to love you both. Will you not stay here and help my old wife, and when your son grows up he shall go fishing with me?"

The queen wished for nothing better. She was still frightened that someone might find her and her baby, and slay them. So she agreed to stay with the old couple and let her boy grow up in the fisherman's cottage.

"What is your child's name?" asked the fisherman's wife.

"He has no name," said the queen, who was not going to say that he was Prince Lamonides. "We will call him little Nemo!"

Nemo means Nobody, and under that curious name the little boy grew up.

He was a fine child, sturdy and handsome. Everyone loved him, all the other children of the island followed him and made him their leader.

"Nemo is our king!" they cried. "Nemo is our brave and valiant king!"

His mother heard them calling this,

and she smiled proudly to think that Nemo should show his kingship even on such a poor and desolate island.

Now one day, when Nemo had grown into a strong and handsome youth, strange news came to the little island. It was brought by some visiting traders, who had been to the land which the queen had once ruled over.

"We have a fearful story to tell," said the traders, as they sat round a huge fire on the beach that night, eating and drinking with all the fishermen. "Have

you heard of the great sea-dragon that once came to these coasts and brought fear and trembling to all men?"

"We have heard of it," answered the men.

"It has come once again," said the traders. "We ourselves saw it not four weeks back. It was a fearsome thing, long and scaly, with spines along its back, and it made a noise like the clashing of great stones one upon the other."

The listening fishermen turned pale.

"Will it visit our islands?" they asked.

"We do not know," answered the traders. "It is causing terror in the land that lies beyond your islands, two days distant. There it demands a young maiden every day, and if it is not obeyed, it crawls upon the land and breaks down houses and castles as easily as a wave smashes shells."

"Does no one fight this sea-dragon?" asked Nemo.

"Oh, yes, but none has yet lived to tell the tale," said the traders. "It is said that soon the dragon will demand the king's own daughter."

"Surely that will be refused!" cried the listeners.

"Not so," said the traders. "The people hate their king, and will demand that his daughter suffers as theirs have done."

When the traders had gone, Nemo thought about their strange story, and the more he thought of it the greater was his wish to try his luck against the dragon. He was very strong, and was growing tired of the dull life of the fisherman. So one day he went to his mother and told her what he meant to do.

She was afraid when she thought of her son going back to the land where his father had been king, but she dare not tell him this, in case he should demand the throne itself. She was filled with fear also, to think that Nemo should wish to fight the terrible dragon.

But nothing she could say would stop the boy.

"I will kill the dragon, win gold for myself, and come back to you a rich man," he said to her, when he kissed her goodbye and set off in his little boat, a sword and shield beside him.

For a whole day he sailed, then a great storm came and blew him many miles off course, so that he did not know where he was. He sailed on for three more days without seeing land, and then at last he saw a small island, green and beautiful, lying to the west.

He landed there, and looked to see if

there were any people who could tell him
where he was. Presently he saw a group
of lovely maidens coming to meet him,
with a woman who looked like a goddess
leading them. They greeted him kindly,
and took him to a cave which was hung
with rich cloths and adorned with golden
couches.

"You are Prince Lamonides, are you
not?" said the goddess. "We saw that you
were coming by gazing into our crystal
ball, in which we see all the future."

139

"Nay," said Nemo in surprise. "I am no prince. I am merely Nemo, a fisher-lad. I go to kill the great sea-dragon that ravages the land beyond the outermost islands."

The maidens smiled when they heard him say that he was a fisher-lad, for they thought that it was his modesty. They were pleased with the courteous, handsome youth, with his modest ways, and the goddess made much of him.

"Well, we will call you Nemo, if that is your wish," she said, smiling. "But pray let us give you advice, if you go to kill the dragon. He cannot be slain on land, nor can anyone hope to conquer him in the water, which is the monster's own domain."

"How, then, can he be killed?" asked Nemo, puzzled.

"From the air," answered the goddess. "We will give you winged anklets and a winged helmet, and with these you can fly above the waters, and strike the monster from the air."

The maidens fetched a wonderful

helmet which had wings sprouting from
each side, and they placed it on Nemo's
head. Then they gave him winged anklets
and bade him buckle them on. This he
did, and then found, to his amazement
and delight, that he could fly with ease
into the air, as gently as a bird. He
thanked the goddess and her maidens,
and then, leaving his little boat on the
shore, he flew straight up into the sky.

For a day and a half he kept on his way, and at last reached the land he sought. It was a country of sadness and mourning, for many young maidens had been devoured by the sea-dragon. Nemo saw a procession wending its way to the shore, and he flew down to see what it was.

At the head walked the king, weeping into his hands. Behind him, bound, came his beautiful daughter, pale but brave. Following were the people, silent and stern. Nemo asked an old man where the procession was going.

"The people are going to bind the princess to the dragon's rock," he answered. "They do this because they hate the king, not because they wish to slay the maiden. Ever since the king took the throne from our old ruler, nineteen years ago, there has been grief and misery here, for he has been cruel and hard to us. This is their revenge."

Nemo looked with pity on the pale maiden, and determined to save her if he could. He watched two men take her

to a rock and bind her there. She did not struggle, but stood bravely erect.

The people went to a high cliff, and stayed there in silence watching for the dragon, who came every day at noon. Nemo watched, too.

Suddenly, far out to sea, there came a stirring of white foam, and the people pointed at it and shouted: "The dragon comes! The dragon comes!"

Nearer and nearer came the monster. Nemo could see its long scaly body, and its fierce head which it held high above the water. It moved like a serpent, lashing the water with its tail as it came.

All the people watched it, pale with

fear. They did not see Nemo suddenly fly from the ground and dart upwards like a swallow. Nor did they hear the flutter of his winged anklets, for the king was wailing loudly.

Nemo flew towards the dragon. He held his shield and sword in his hands, and his heart leaped at the thought of the fight to come. Suddenly there came a shout from the watching people. They had seen him.

"What is it? A bird? An eagle? One of the gods? Oh, what is it? Surely he is a rescuer!"

So came the shouts, and Nemo heard them and was glad. Soon he was directly over the dragon, and he darted down and struck at its fierce head. The monster saw the flash of his sword and jerked away, so that Nemo struck him lightly on the neck and gave him but a scratch.

But this was enough to anger him, and the dragon let forth a roar that deafened the people, and shook the very clouds above.

Nemo leaped upwards out of the

dragon's way as soon as his stroke had missed, and it was as well he had. For the beast lashed out with his tail with such force that the sea was churned into water-spouts and great waves that sprang upwards to the sky.

Nemo waited until the waters had calmed down again, and then he darted downwards once more.

This time he flew behind the creature's head, and tried to cut it off with one great stroke. But the dragon saw him, and snapped swiftly at the youth's arm. Nemo drew it back just in time, and flew upwards, slashing at the monster's tail as he did so. He cut the tip right off, and in pain and anger the dragon raised himself out of the waters and tried to seize Nemo's feet.

But the lad was far too quick for him, and smote the dragon on the mouth so that it bled and made the water red all round. Once again the monster roared with rage, and great rocks split in half at the sound, and fell from the cliffs. The sea tossed and foamed, causing Nemo to

lose sight of the dragon.

He saw him again a moment later, swimming swiftly towards the rock where the princess was bound. At once the youth flew after him, and shouted loudly. The dragon stopped angrily and snapped at Nemo as he came down like a hawk alighting on its prey.

But the youth was wary and waited until the dragon was tired of snapping. Then with one great stroke he smote the monster's head and severed it from his body, so that it fell into the sea and sank from sight.

Then there went up such a cry from the watching people that surely it was heard from one end of the world to the other.

Nemo flew to the rock where the princess was held prisoner, and quickly cut her bonds. Taking her in his arms, he flew to the shore and met the hurrying people.

What a victory that was! How everyone praised the youth and loaded him with riches! Even the king himself fell down at Nemo's feet and kissed them, so glad was he to get his daughter back again. The youth was taken to the palace and there for three days he was feasted and made much of.

He fell in love with the beautiful princess and she with him. The king consented to their marriage, although

he thought the youth was but a fisher-
lad. But he held himself in such a
princely manner and behaved himself so
well that none could believe him to be
but a poor fisherman.

"I would like to fetch my mother to
see my wedding," said Nemo. So the king
gave him consent to fetch her, and the
youth set off in a fine ship given to him
by the grateful people.

Imagine his mother's astonishment
when Nemo arrived in this ship, and told
her that he was going to marry the
daughter of her old enemy who had killed
her husband. Little did Nemo know that
he was the rightful king, and his mother
determined that not yet would she tell
him.

She set sail with him in the ship, and veiled herself heavily so that none should see her face. Soon they came to the land where she had once been queen, and she was taken in a chariot to the palace where she had lived so happily for many years.

She greeted the king still with her veil on, so that he did not know her. Then she retired to her room to prepare for the grand wedding.

When the hour came, the youth proudly rode in state beside his lovely bride. The king followed and behind him, in a carriage by herself, rode Nemo's mother – with her veil off!

Then the people knew her, and cried out in amazement and gladness. They ran to her carriage, calling, "The queen! Queen! What miracle is this! Where is your son?"

Then all the carriages stopped, and the king stood up in astonishment that quickly turned to fear when he saw that the wife of the man he had killed was riding behind him. He could not

understand it – surely she was drowned,
and her son, long ago.

"Where is your son, where is he?" cried
the people. And Cleo stood up and
pointed to where Nemo stood.

"There he is," she said. "There is your
rightful king!"

The nobles ran to Nemo and knelt
before him. The people shouted for joy,
for they had never forgotten their old
king, and they hated their new one.

As for that wicked man himself, he was terrified. It had all happened so suddenly and so strangely that he felt as if he must be in a dream.

Four nobles rushed to his carriage and flung open the door. They took the trembling man roughly by the arms, and dragged him to the market place, where all the people assembled in excitement.

"Have mercy!" he groaned.

"You had no mercy on Teleus, nor on Cleo and her baby!" said the nobles sternly. "How can you ask for mercy

now? You will be ordered to die, for Lamonides will avenge his father's death by yours, be sure of that!"

The unhappy man was bound by ropes, and stood in front of all the people, afraid and ashamed. None spoke a good word for him, for to none had he been kind or gracious.

"Surely, surely, it is a dream!" he thought.

But it was no dream. The crown was taken from his head, and before Nemo was wedded to the lovely princess, he was made king of his own country, and hailed as Lamonides, son of Teleus and Cleo, ruler of the land from north to south, from east to west!

Lamonides, happy and amazed at his good fortune, turned to where his bride's father stood trembling, bound by ropes.

"Loose him," he commanded. "I will spare his life for the sake of his daughter who is now my wife. He can do no more harm."

So with a merciful deed to begin his kingship, Nemo, now King Lamonides, began to rule with his fair wife. Many long years was he on the throne, happy and contented for the rest of his days.

What Faces
They Made!

"Oh, you two bad teddies!" said the teddy bears' mother one morning. "How you quarrel and fight! Now shake paws and make it up – go along, do as you're told."

"I'm not going to shake paws with a horrid bear like Bruiny," said Tubby, and he turned his back.

"And I am never going to smile at Tubby again," said Bruiny.

"I can't think how it is I've got such a nasty brother as Bruiny," said Tubby. "I don't feel as if I shall ever speak to him again."

"Ma! That's how he's always talking about me!" said Bruiny. "Smack him!"

Bruiny frowned at Tubby, and Tubby put out his tongue. Their mother looked at them both. What was she to do with them? She had smacked them often. She had sent them to bed. She had taken away their Saturday treats. But still they frowned and squabbled and wouldn't play together properly.

Then she had an idea. "Come here," she said firmly to them both. "Now you, Bruiny, sit on this little chair – and you, Tubby, sit on this one – just opposite him. That's right. Now do you know what you are to do?"

"No, Ma. What?" said the little bears, sulkily. They sat opposite to one another, but they wouldn't look at each other at all.

"You're to take it in turn to make nasty faces at one another," said their mother. "Really horrible. You can begin first, Bruiny. Think hard what face you are going to make, and then make it. Tubby must watch you, but neither of you must say a word.

"Then, Tubby must think of what nasty face he is going to make, and he must make it, and you must watch him, Bruiny. As you always seem to want to be

horrid to one another, I am sure you will have a most enjoyable morning being really unpleasant."

"Ha!" thought Bruiny. "This is good! I shall make my pop-eye face. Tubby hates that!" So he opened his eyes wide, rolled them round and round, and opened his mouth too. He looked dreadful.

Tubby watched him. "Not much of a face!" he thought. "Silly fellow! Can't even make a good face at me. Ah – I'll make a beauty – a really dreadful one."

He did. He pricked up his little ears, he squinted, and he put out his tongue and waggled it. It really looked more funny than rude, though. Bruiny suddenly wanted to laugh. He was quite shocked with himself – fancy wanting to laugh at that horrid Tubby.

Then Bruiny thought of another face. He sucked his fat cheeks in and shut his eyes until there was nothing of them left. Then he waggled his nose.

Tubby giggled, and then turned his giggle into a cough. That really was a funny face – not a bit rude or horrid. He thought of another one himself.

He blew out one cheek but not the other and shut one eye and kept the other open. Then he pressed his snubby little nose up with his paw. He looked too comical for words.

Bruiny burst into a loud laugh. His mother heard him. "Bruiny!" she said. "I told you to be horrible, not to begin laughing. Now go on with your unkind faces please, and don't make a joke of it."

"But Ma – I can't think of any more faces," said Bruiny.

"Well, sit and make the same ones at each other again," said his mother. "You and Tubby often spend the whole morning making faces and squabbling – you ought to be glad I'm not scolding you for it today, but I am letting you sit till lunch-time and be horrid to one another."

She went out of the room. Tubby

immediately made another peculiar face, and Bruiny almost fell off his chair with laughing. "Oh, Tubby – that was a wonderful face!" he said. "How did you do it?"

"I'll show you," said Tubby, pleased. "You do this – and then this – and then that!"

Bruiny squealed with laughter again. "You look like a goat or something," he said. "You do make wonderful faces, Tubby. Much better than mine."

"Oh, well – you can do jigsaws long before I do," said Tubby generously, and he smiled. Bruiny looked at him.

"That wasn't a face, was it?" he said. "That smile, I mean. That was nice. I liked it."

"I say – it's a dreadful bore to have to sit here all morning and make faces, isn't it?" said Tubby. "I rather wanted to build a garage for our little motor-cars."

"Oooh – that would be nice," said Bruiny. "But Ma says we've got to sit here and be horrible to each other."

"I don't feel as if I want to be, now,"

said Tubby. "You don't either. Let's ask Ma if we can get down and play."

So they asked her. She looked at them sternly. "Well, I really don't understand you. It seemed to me this morning as if the only thing you wanted to do was to be nasty to one another – and so I sat you down and told you to be. Now you tell me you want to be friends and play together."

"Yes," said Tubby and Bruiny, beginning to slide off their chairs.

"Now, you listen to me," said their mother. "I'll let you get down and play with each other – but if you want to be horrible and call each other names, and squabble, you must come and tell me. And I'll say yes, you can if you like – but you must come back and sit on these chairs opposite one another to be horrid. You can take it in turn then and it will be fair."

"Yes, Ma," said both little bears, and they ran to get their bricks to build a garage.

They were both so afraid of having to go and sit on their chairs and take turns at being horrid that they played happily all the morning.

I think their mother was rather clever, don't you?

If you squabble a lot, you'd better not let your mother read this story – or you know what will happen to you!

The Magic
Knitting-Needles

Mother Click-Clack had a wonderful pair of knitting-needles. You should just have seen them!

All she had to do was to set them by a ball of wool and say, "Click-clack, now, needles, let me hear you click-clack!"

And at once those needles would set to work knitting all by themselves. They flew in and out, making a clickity-clackity noise rather like two or three clocks ticking away at once. The ball of wool unwound quickly as the needles pulled at it, and very soon Mother Click-Clack would see a long stocking made, or a baby's bonnet, or a child's jersey. It was really marvellous.

One day she lent her magic knitting-needles to Sally Simple. Sally had got all behind with her knitting, so she was very pleased to have the needles.

"When the needles have made what you want, bring them straight back to me," said Mother Click-Clack. "Don't leave them about, whatever you do, especially not near wool. Bring them straight back."

"Very well, Mother Click-Clack," said Sally. So off she went with the silvery needles, delighted to think her knitting would so soon be done. She fetched a ball of blue wool and three balls of white. She wanted a little coat for her sister's baby.

"Click-clack, now, needles," she said. "Click-clack, I want a baby's coat."

The needles set to work at once. They flew in and out, making a fine click-clackety noise. The balls of wool unwound quickly, and lo and behold, Sally Simple saw a baby's blue and white coat being made before her very eyes. It was really marvellous! It didn't take longer than ten minutes to do.

Now, as you know, Sally Simple had

promised to take the magic needles straight back to Mother Click-Clack when she had finished with them. But Sally had a bad memory and didn't always do what she said she would.

She didn't take the needles back. No – she so very badly wanted to take the blue-and-white coat to show her sister that she forgot all about her promise. What did it matter anyway! She would only be about an hour at her sister's.

She put on her hat, took up the dear little coat and ran off. She left the magic needles by themselves on the table – and, do you know, quite near them was Sally's great basket of wools!

There were balls of brown wool for knitting stockings, balls of black wool for socks, balls of blue wool for coats and bonnets, balls of white wool for vests, and all kind of odd balls for things like scarves and mittens.

The magic needles lay quietly for a minute or two. Then they gave a little jump towards the basket of wools. They gave another little jump – and another – and then they landed right into the middle of the basket.

Ah! This is wonderful! The needles had seldom had so much wool to work with. They began to fly in and out

merrily. The balls of wool jumped and jerked as the wool unwound from them. *Clickety-clackety, clickety-clackety, clickety-clackety* went those needles.

Now as the needles hadn't been told what to make, they just made what they thought. The first things they made were two pairs of brown stockings for the legs of the kitchen table.

As soon as the stockings were finished, they flew to the legs of the table and slipped themselves on. My, they did look splendid!

Then the needles began to work with the blue wool – a bonnet for the clock. Fancy that!

The bonnet was soon made. It even had two knitted ribbons to tie it tightly. It flew to the clock and put itself neatly on the top, tying the ribbons in a neat bow. Dear dear! Whatever next!

The needles clickety-clacked at the white wool. Vests for the chairs next. Aha! How warm the chairs would be wearing woollen vests! It didn't take those needles long to make four long white vests. They flew off to the chairs and put themselves on at once. How nice and warm they were!

This time the needles knitted the pink wool and the yellow wool together and made a long scarf for the dog who was lying peacefully by the fire. Wasn't he surprised to find a warm scarf suddenly knotting itself round his neck! He did look smart!

The cat walked into the kitchen at that moment and the needles clicked merrily in the blue wool. They made a blue dress for the cat and a blue bonnet. Puss miaowed in surprise when she found them on her back and head. She did look funny in them! She sat down in her basket and wondered how to get them off.

The magic needles knitted black socks for the stool, and a coat for the coal-scuttle. They knitted one long stocking for the poker and a petticoat for the lamp. They knitted a pink coat for the grandfather clock, with a pink bonnet to match. The grandfather clock didn't

like them. After all, it was a grandfather, not a baby! But it had to wear them.

Then the needles started on a jersey for the piano, with leggings to match. This was a very big job and the needles clicked hard. *Clickety-clack, clickety-clack, clickety-clack, clickety-clack!* they went.

And in the middle of it all, Sally Simple came back.

"Now, where are those knitting needles?" she said. "I must take them back to Mother Click-Clack."

Clickety-clack, clickety-clack! went the needles busily. Sally Simple stared at her wool basket – there was hardly any wool left. Wherever had it gone?

Then she looked round the room – and oh, how she stared at the sights she saw!

"The dog's got a scarf round his neck! The cat's got a dress and bonnet on!" cried Sally.

Clickety-clack, said the busy needles.

"My goodness! The table's got stockings! And the stool has got socks! And the coal-scuttle is wearing a coat! Bless us all! Look at that!" cried Sally in dismay.

"Oh, look at the lamp – it's wearing a woollen petticoat! And the grandfather clock has got a pink bonnet and coat! What's this on the poker – mercy me, a stocking! And the chairs have got vests and the clock's got a bonnet! Oh, why did I leave those needles near my wool!"

She went to take them – and at the same moment they finished the jersey and leggings for the piano. They shot to the piano and put themselves on – dear

me, how very strange the piano looked!

Sally Simple snatched up the needles and ran off to Mother Click-Clack with them. She was almost in tears.

"Your horrid, horrid needles have knitted up all my balls of wool!" she said. "They've made a dress and bonnet for the cat – and stockings for the table-legs – and …"

Mother Click-Clack began to laugh. "Oh, Sally, you'll be the death of me!" she laughed. "Fancy letting the needles do all that! Didn't I tell you to bring them back as soon as you'd finished with them? I know their little ways."

"Now I've got to undo all those silly vests and stockings and socks and bonnets," cried Sally Simple. "It will take me ages!"

"Well, I'm sorry, Sally," said Mother Click-Clack. "But it's your own fault. You should give back things you've borrowed as soon as ever you can."

Poor Sally Simple. She's still undoing the jersey and leggings that the needles made for the piano.

Billy and the
West Wind

Billy's mother was very unhappy. When Billy came home from school she had tears in her eyes and she was hunting all over the place for something.

"What's the matter, Mum?" asked Billy in surprise, for he thought that grown-ups never cried.

"I've lost my lovely diamond ring," said his mother. "It's the one your daddy gave me years ago, and I love it best of all my rings. It was loose and it must have dropped off. Now I can't find it anywhere, and I'm so unhappy about it."

"I'll help you to look for it," said Billy, at once. "Just tell me all the places you've been this morning, Mum."

"I had it on at breakfast time," said his mother. "Then I went to see old Mrs

Brown who lives at the far edge of the meadow. I may have dropped it on my way there, of course. Perhaps you'd like to go and look on the path, Billy."

So off Billy ran, his eyes looking all over the ground as he went. It was very windy, and the grass kept blowing about, which made it very difficult to see the ground properly. He soon came to the meadow and then he went down on his hands and knees and began to look very carefully indeed. He did so want to find that ring!

Suddenly he saw a small figure dart quickly behind a bush. It was too big for a rabbit and too small to be one of his friends about to play a trick on him. What could it be? He peeped round the bush and what do you think he found, hiding there?

It was a small elf, with wide, frightened eyes and tiny, pointed ears! Now Billy had never in his life seen an elf and he stared in surprise.

"Please don't hurt me!" said the elf, in a little tinkling voice.

"Of course I won't!" said Billy. "But where are your wings? I thought all elves had wings and could fly."

"Well, I usually do have wings," said the little creature, who was clothed in a beautiful suit of purple and blue. "They are lovely silver ones, and I took them off this morning to clean them. I put them down on that bush there, and the wind came along and blew them away. Now I'm looking everywhere for them, but I can't find them anywhere. It's too awful!"

"I'm looking for something too," said Billy. "I'm hunting for my mother's diamond ring. Have you seen it?"

"No," said the elf. "But I can easily get it for you, if you'll help me find my wings."

"Could you really?" said Billy, excitedly. "But how am I to help you?"

"You could go to the West Wind and ask him what he's done with my wings," said the elf. "I can't do it myself because I'm afraid of him – he's so big and blustery – but you are big and tall so perhaps you wouldn't mind."

"What an adventure this is turning out to be!" thought Billy to himself, feeling more and more excited.

"Of course I will help you," said Billy to the elf. "But wherever will I find the West Wind? I didn't even know it was a person!"

"Oh, goodness!" said the elf, laughing. "He's very much a person, I can tell you. He's gone to see his cousin, the Rainbow Lady, on the top of Blowaway Hill."

"Where's that?" asked Billy. "Tell me, and I'll go straight away."

"Well, the quickest way is to find the tower in the wood," said the elf, pointing down a little rabbit-path through some trees. "It has two doors. Go in the one that faces the sun. Shut it. Wish that you could be in the same place as the West Wind. Open the other door and you'll find yourself there! Then just ask the West Wind what he's done with my wings and tell him he really must let me have them back."

Billy waved goodbye and ran off down the narrow little path. He had never been down it before. After a while he came to a tall, thin tower among the trees. Billy walked all round it. It looked very strange

indeed. There were no windows, but there were two small round doors. One faced the sun and the other was in shadow, just as the elf had described.

Billy opened the sunny door and walked boldly through. The tower was high, dark, and cold inside. Shivering, Billy shut the door behind him and found himself in black darkness, just like night! He felt a little frightened, but he remembered what the elf had said and shouted, "I wish I was on the top of Blowaway Hill."

He heard a faint rushing sound and the tower rocked very slightly. Billy opened the other door and daylight streamed into the strange tower, making him blink. He walked out of the door – and how surprised he was!

He was no longer in the wood – he was on the top of a sunny hill, and in front of him was a small, pretty cottage, overgrown with honeysuckle.

"This must be the Rainbow Lady's house," thought Billy. He marched up the little path and knocked at the door.

A voice called, "Come in!" So Billy turned the handle …

A draught of cold air blew on him as soon as he stepped inside. He shivered and looked round in surprise. Two people were sitting drinking lemonade at a little round table. A fire burned brightly in one corner and a grey cat sat washing itself on the rug. Everything seemed quite ordinary until he looked at the people there!

One was the Rainbow Lady. She was very beautiful and her dress was so

bright that Billy blinked his eyes when he looked at her. She was dressed in all the colours of the rainbow, and her dress floated out around her like a mist. Her eyes shone like two stars.

The other person was the West Wind. He was fat and blustery, and his breath came in great gusts as if he had been running very hard. It was his breathing that made the big windy draughts that blew round the little room. His clothes were like April clouds and blew out round him all the time. Billy was so astonished to see him that at first he couldn't say a word.

"Well! What do you want?" asked the West Wind in a gusty voice. As he spoke Billy felt a shower of raindrops fall on him. It was very strange.

"I've come from the little elf who lives down in the meadow," said Billy. "She says you took away her wings this morning, West Wind, and she does so badly want them back."

"Dear me!" said the West Wind, surprised, and as he spoke another shower of raindrops fell on Billy's head. "How was I to know they belonged to the elf? I thought they had been put there by someone who didn't want them! I knew the red goblin was wanting a pair of wings so I blew them to him!"

"Oh dear!" said Billy, in dismay. "What a pity! The elf is really very upset. She can't fly, you see. She only took them off to clean them."

"West Wind, you are always doing silly things like that," said the Rainbow Lady, in a soft voice. "One day you will get into trouble. You had better go to the red goblin and ask for those wings back."

"Oh, no, I can't do that," said the West Wind, looking very uncomfortable and puffing more raindrops all over the room.

Billy looked round to see if there was an umbrella anywhere. It was not very nice to have showers of rain falling all over him whenever the West Wind spoke. He found an umbrella in a corner and put it up over himself.

"Oh, yes, you *can* go and get the wings back," said the Rainbow Lady, and she said it so firmly that the West Wind eventually agreed. He got up, took Billy's hand and went sulkily out of the door. He had a very cold, wet hand, but Billy didn't mind. It was very exciting.

The West Wind took Billy down the hill at such a pace that the little boy gasped for breath. They came to a river and the West Wind jumped straight across it, dragging Billy with him. Then he rushed across some fields and at last came to a small, lopsided house. A tiny goblin sat in the garden with a schoolbook, crying bitterly. The West Wind took no notice of the little creature but walked quickly up and knocked on the door.

"Stay here," he said to Billy, and left him in the garden. The little boy went over to the goblin.

"What's the matter?" he asked. The little goblin looked up. He had a quaint, pointed face and different coloured eyes – one was green and the other was yellow.

"I can't do my homework," he said. "Look! It's taking-away sums and this one won't take away."

Billy looked – and then he smiled – for the silly little goblin had put the sum down wrong! He had to take 18 from 81, and he had written the sum upside down so that he was trying to take 81 away from 18. No wonder it wouldn't come right!

Billy put the sum down right for him and the goblin did it easily. He was so grateful.

"Is there anything else I can help you with?" Billy asked kindly.

"Well," said the goblin, shyly, "I never can remember which is my right hand and which is my left, and I'm always getting into dreadful trouble at school because of that. I suppose you can't tell me the best way to remember which hand is which?"

"Oh, that's easy!" said Billy at once. "The hand you are writing with is your right hand, and the one that's left is the left one, of course!"

"Oh, that's wonderful!" said the little goblin, in delight. "I shall never forget now. I always know which hand I write with, so I shall always know my right hand and the other one must be the left. Right hand, left hand, right hand, left hand!"

Just at that moment the door of the little house flew open and out came the West Wind in a fearful temper.

"That miserable red goblin won't give me back those wings!" he roared, and a whole shower of rain fell heavily on poor Billy and his new goblin friend. "So we can't have them!"

Billy stared in dismay. Now he wouldn't be able to take them to the elf and she wouldn't give him his mother's ring! It was too bad. He looked so upset that the small goblin he had just helped gently took hold of his hand.

"What's the matter?" he asked. "Do you want those silver wings that the West Wind gave my father this morning? They were really for me to learn to fly on, but if you badly want them, you shall have them back. You've been so kind to me! I'd like to do something in return!"

"Oh, would you let me have the wings?" said Billy, in delight. The little goblin said nothing but ran indoors. He came out with a pair of glittering silver wings and gave them to Billy. The little boy thanked him joyfully and turned to go. The West Wind took his hand and back they went to Blowaway Hill again.

"Well, you never know when a little kindness is going to bring you a big reward!" said the West Wind, in a jolly voice. "It's a good thing you helped that little goblin, isn't it?"

"Oh, yes," said Billy happily. "Now I must get back to the meadow again and give these wings to the elf."

But when he turned to look, he was dismayed to see that the tower had disappeared.

"Oh no!" he cried. "The tower has gone! However am I to get back home?"

Poor Billy! It was quite true – the magic tower had gone and could not take him back to the wood as he had planned! But luckily the Rainbow Lady was watching through the window and came out to see what was wrong.

"Don't worry," she said when Billy explained what had happened. "Just put on these elf wings, and the West Wind will blow you gently through the air back to the meadow."

The Rainbow Lady took the wings from Billy and clipped them neatly on to his shoulders.

"Now!" she said, turning to the West Wind. "I said *gently*, so please don't be rough. Remember your manners for once!"

189

Then Billy felt himself rising into the air, higher and higher, until he was far above the hill. His wings beat gently backwards and forwards and the West Wind blew him swiftly along. It was a most wonderful feeling.

"This is the most marvellous adventure I shall ever have!" said Billy, joyfully. "Oh, how I wish I always had wings! It is lovely to fly like this!"

The West Wind smiled and remembered his manners and did not blow too roughly. Soon Billy could see the meadow far below and the two of them started to glide gently downwards.

The West Wind said goodbye and left Billy on the edge of wood. He soon found a path he knew and ran along to the bush where he had seen the elf. She was still there waiting for him.

When she saw that Billy had her wings on his back she cried out in delight and ran to meet him.

She unclipped her wings from Billy's shoulders and put them on her own. "Oh, thank you, thank you!" she cried.

"Could you give me my mother's ring now?" asked Billy. "You said you would if I helped you."

"Of course!" said the elf. "While you were gone I set all the rabbits in the wood hunting for me – and one of them brought me this lovely shining ring. Is it your mother's?"

Of course, it was! So Billy ran all the way home and when he showed his mother the ring she could hardly believe her eyes.

"You are clever to find it!" she said.

"I didn't find it – a rabbit found it," said Billy. But his mother didn't believe him, and when he told her his adventure she said he really must have been dreaming!

So next week he is going to ask that elf to come to tea with him – and then everyone will know it wasn't a dream! I wish I was going for tea with them, too, don't you?